Missing Persons

Missing Persons

by
Carole Giangrande

CORMORANT BOOKS

Copyright © Carole Giangrande, 1994

Published with the assistance of the Canada Council and the Ontario Arts Council.

"Missing Persons" and "Hard News" were first published in *Grain*, "Beirut Garden" in *New Quarterly*, "Love and the Gentle Art of Flying" in *Descant*, "Moonwalkers" in *Matrix*, and "Into The Fire" in *Canadian Forum*. "The Memory Wall" will be published in *New Quarterly*, Winter 1994.

The author wishes to acknowledge the support of the Ontario Arts Council and the Banff Centre for the Arts in the writing of this book. She would also like to thank Brian Gibson for what he has given to this work by his friendship, patience, and generous spirit.

Edited by Gena K. Gorrell.

Cover art from a 1968 rice paper on wood, *The Descent II*, by Richard Ciccimarra, courtesy of Ciccimarra's estate, from the collection of the Art Gallery of Greater Victoria.

Cover design by Artcetera Graphics Inc.

Author photograph by Donna Moyseuik.

Published by
Cormorant Books Inc., RR 1, Dunvegan, Ontario K0C 1J0.

Printed and bound in Canada.

Canadian Cataloguing in Publication Data
Giangrande, Carole, 1945-
    Missing persons
ISBN 0-920953-63-8
    I. Title.
PS8563.I24M48 1994   C813' .54   C94-900009-4
PR9199.3.G43M48 1994

In memory of bpNichol

CONTENTS

Missing Persons 9
Beirut Garden 23
Hard News 36
What History Teaches 38
Love and the Gentle Art of Flying 54
Moonwalkers 69
This Is For Mandy 80
The Memory Wall 82
Into the Fire 97
How, If Ever, the Story Ends 112

MISSING PERSONS

First the letters stopped coming, the ones in brown envelopes, the addresses scribbled out three times and the old stamps torn off so you figured they had made the trip across Canada more times than Via Rail; those letters from the old log farmhouse in the Kootenays didn't come any more, and I missed them so terribly, I was almost ashamed to say. So that was the first I knew something was wrong, or maybe I'm telling the story backwards; maybe the phone part came first, me dialling the number, hearing a phone purr a long, lonely way off on the other side of the Rockies and that funny tin voice like someone with a bad cold, the number you have reached is out of service. And nobody at Bell Canada, not one damn operator in this whole, big barn of a country had ever heard of Elizabeth and Gordon; they just went and dropped off the face of the earth, disappeared.

All I got were blank looks when I asked around. Thought you'd kept in touch, my friends would say, and after a while I'd feel embarrassed, lower my eyes, sure they'd figure I'd done something awful; Elizabeth and

Gordon were friendly people; they wouldn't cut me off without a reason.

So they weren't answering my letters, and that had gone on close to six months. Now I'm not much with words, I know that; Elizabeth said to me once, Bonnie, talking's not your strong suit, you throw words like bricks. So okay, I sent them both some of the photos in my new exhibit, the ones of the dead maple leaves floating in the dead lakes; also a note saying tell me what you think of them, because for sure Elizabeth would have lots to say about how she hates polluters, and that would make her write. Then I figured maybe she was waiting for her bank statement to come so she could write to me on the back of it, because she's into recycling, and that was what the holdup was. Just to be on the safe side, I told her, if I said something wrong, I'm sorry; Celine and I both miss you. She's sixteen years old now, and she wonders when we'll visit you in British Columbia. That isn't true; Celine couldn't care less.

Maybe Elizabeth knew this was a lie, figured everything else was a lie too. I keep forgetting how she hates lies.

Still, you have these reflexes, and every day I trudge downstairs to the mailbox. I live in a flat over a hardware store on Queen Street in downtown Toronto. The mailboxes are in a narrow corridor in the front entrance, the flat-against-the-wall kind of mailboxes with little daisy-petal holes stamped into each one, so you can see if you got real mail or just junk flyers from Shoppers Drug Mart. The super's wife polishes the old brass on the boxes to a high shine, but the whole row of them got dented in one night by a drunk. So there's my face in the mailbox all stretched out of shape, my nose melting into a runaway chin, my long, sandy hair bent and frazzled like a thousand tiny twigs in a windstorm; not surprising that I kind of look perplexed. Except for my eyes; I watch them look out at me from a flat part of the mailbox that didn't get smashed. Big hazel eyes, real nice eyes, Allan used to say to me; only they prowl over everything like a pair of wild animals; only now they go and stare back at me with such a stupid longing for God knows what that I feel ashamed, just as if I was doing something wrong, feeling that way and not being able to hide it.

The keyhole of the mailbox sits right in the middle of one reflected eye. I ram the key into the slot, watch it break my eye in half. Then I open the box—flyers and a Hydro bill—that's all; let the palm of my hand roam along the inside, the way you would if you were blind and feeling around for something.

Behind me the front door bangs and I jump. Celine's come in out of nowhere, slouching against the wall, her leather jacket hanging from her shoulders like loose skin. She has Allan's black hair, short and straight, blunt-cut, his pale white solemn face; she's painted her thin lips bright red. But her dark eyes, so dark they seem to eat up light, those are her own. When she looks right at me, there's a tight little smile on her face.

"Mooning over the mail again?" she remarks.

Not hello or anything. If you can feel naked inside your head, that's how I feel right then; naked, just as if she's stuck in her hand and yanked my soul out. I slam the box shut. Celine smiles faintly, turns her back, and trots upstairs, her boots thunking on the bare wood. Already she has that smug look, like she doesn't need anyone.

Upstairs she pulls out her key and strides into my flat; she acts as if she has a right to the place, even though she moved out a few months back because she can't stand my smoking. No kidding, she stares at the ashtrays full of butts, the dirty dishes in the sink; I swear she was born to be a goddamn health inspector. Then she slouches against the wall, eyeballing me, arms crossed. She looks defiant, still wearing her jacket, but her eyes are a little fearful; maybe she's surprised she got away with being such a smartass.

"I'm from the *Guinness Book of Records*," she snaps. "How long you been livin' in pigshit now, six months?"

I don't answer. Six months doing a show, I think to myself; trying to forget Allan, dead two years, and Elizabeth and Gordon, who cleared out not long after from the house we'd all shared since you were just a kid, Celine, and that's pretty well half my life gone; six months of nonstop work, coffee, butts and Big Macs; living in dirty flannel shirts hanging loose to hide a spread of flab around the middle because I hardly ever go for walks any more; my ratty jeans tight around the bottom, hair loose and straggling out of an old metal clip, an unlit cigarette dangling from my mouth, wire-rimmed glasses held together with Scotch tape; inside me, there's a sheet of ice full of cracks and splinters; I can feel it banging around, damn near ready to break.

I'm scared to come apart in front of Celine. I suck in my lower lip hard and ask her if she's seen my matches.

Her eyes gleam as she walks towards me, her boots clunk-clunking on the hardwood floor. Before I can stop her, she thrusts out her arm and yanks the unlit cigarette from my mouth. I clap my hands to my lips in surprise, but her eyes light up because she's really got me now. She smiles.

"Knock it off, Celine," I start to say, only I know she won't, because she can't; she's only a kid and she knows I owe her something. I don't feel like fighting back for one lousy smoke, or for much of anything, which is her point, I guess.

So she's staring at the wall covered with black-and-white photos, a real sullen look on her face, as if she's going to spit at it any minute. How could she know how scared I got when I lost everybody at once, how I stayed up night after night printing up all my old negatives of Elizabeth and Gord and her dad; I locked myself in the darkroom, and when I saw all the light and shadow of their faces swimming in the bath, I felt so tender; you'd think they were being born out of my body and I was giving them life there in the dark. I try to tell Celine that Elizabeth was my best friend, but she just scoffs; some friend, won't have anything to do with you, won't even say why; you're so gone on those pictures, how would you know? She's staring at me now, the hard and angry look gone from her eyes. Just sad, that's all, the way you'd expect your kid to be if you hardly ever talked to her.

"You get off on this," she says, glaring at the photos on the wall. "You don't care about real people."

Her face has lost the hard look, and now I think she's the one who's going to cry. Instead she clunk-clunks out the door, slams it shut; her boots make a hard rhythm going down the stairs. I think of the click of Morse code; someone calling for help. It's the first time in months I've noticed she's hurting.

I feel a flutter in my gut, my heart beating faster;

something running through me like a low hum, an electric current. It's like defrosting a fridge; I can feel myself coming back to life, tingling all over, my fingers, everything. Little by little the feeling grows, that maybe I can fix things up, find out what happened with Elizabeth and Gordon, make it up to Celine. But at the moment, I'm not sure how.

So over I go to the wall; I'm drawn to a large photo of Elizabeth, one I took of her twenty years ago, just after I finished at Ryerson. I guess I'm figuring she might inspire me, since she's done that before. Back when I took the picture, I was doing a spread for an article of hers in the *Star*, which was how we met. She was so beautiful and I remember asking her to sit for a portrait and she laughed at the idea, but her laugh was like spilling water; the sound of it seemed to splash on things and catch the light. She had a quiet smile, amused, as if she had a secret, as if she knew something about you she'd never tell you. She was so poised; you can see that in the picture, how her hair was combed just so, chestnut-coloured, very shiny, straight down to the shoulders, and her eyes, large, deep blue, and very calm. Your camera just kind of fell into those eyes; they seem to have no bottom.

After she saw the portrait, Elizabeth became my friend; she told me I had a wonderful eye for what's inside of people. She wanted to know all about me, but I figured if she liked my portraits that much, I better tell her about the one time I felt sure my picture-taking had unplugged my heart from my brain. I was eighteen, still living just outside Sudbury, working for the *News-Herald*; it was the day the roof of one of the mines collapsed. My dad and my brother Frank both worked at that mine. The paper sent me down to get shots of guys digging through the rubble for victims; my first big Page One story. Now you've got to believe I'd be nervous, but it was more than the job; I could feel a rumble jarring my mind like pebbles coming loose before a rockslide. Christ, I had to call home first, find out if there was any news about Dad and Frank. I tried once, twice; the line was busy. Bet the whole damn town was calling home, getting a buzz-click, that jumpy sound, like even the wires were scared. So I told myself, try again later, first chance you get.

It was pretty exciting doing the story. I let myself fall into the rhythm of the shutter, snap snap like a pair of jaws, my camera hunting for dead and wounded like a vulture with a glass eye. They kept us at a distance, so what could I see? Just rescue workers digging like crazy, the way dogs go after bones, pulling up bodies all caked with dirt and blood. You couldn't make out faces, I swear you couldn't, not a one.

Back in the darkroom I printed up my film, and in my mind I tried to wash away the soot and blood on the shots of miners' bodies; I couldn't even tell who these guys were, but their looks rattled me inside, made me feel like an empty train clattering out of control downhill. And then it hit me. I had family in that mine. I'd been so caught up with my pictures and my first Page One, I'd forgotten to call home again. So I phoned the hospital. My brother Frank had turned up dead. I sat there in shock, staring at this print of a bunch of miners, one poor man who looked like nothing human, squashed like an insect under somebody's boot. What was I supposed to think; this could be my brother for all I knew, I could have said goodbye to him; instead I went and took his fucking picture. I was so stunned I couldn't even cry.

When I told Elizabeth all this, I bawled my head off. She put an arm around me, told me it wasn't my fault what happened, and she reminded me something good came out of it; those photos made the wires and won me a bursary, which is how I got to study in Toronto. She still thought I took fine pictures.

Elizabeth was good at undoing those tight little knots of hurt I never could show to anyone else. For sure I was no talker, so I let her smooth out my words, feed me back my thoughts as if they were warm bread she had just baked, my life the way she wanted me to see it. God, I can't believe how hungry I felt for that. It's not true that no one had ever loved me, but being one of six kids, you just figure you can't take up too much of anyone's time. Finally someone had time for me.

The two of us got so close, like one brain in two bodies. Once she told me I was the eyes and she was the voice, and she smiled when she said it, just as if she couldn't see deep inside of anything without my being there, and I liked that.

Sometimes I'd want to talk to Elizabeth about some trouble I felt in her. There was the fact that she'd wanted kids, had a miscarriage once. She'd talked about it like she'd lost her car keys, no big deal, nothing she'd let me reach in and touch. But it was how she looked at Celine: a sadness that went right into my eyes, straight through my body like a big hard lump of coal down a shaft. I couldn't leave a friend alone with that. So once, after Celine had gone out, I asked Elizabeth what was upsetting her. She shrugged.

"If I knew, I'd tell you," she said.

I couldn't just blurt out, I know you want kids. The words couldn't hold what I saw in her, all those shadows, the place in her body that had given up trying.

"Wish I could help you," I said. Elizabeth laughed.

"You're all eyes, Bonnie. What good's that?"

Christ, what was she saying? Her best friend couldn't help her? So I didn't have the right words, so what.

"My eyes are plenty good," I said to her.

"For what?"

"I'll show you what." I got my camera and told her I wanted to take her picture; how else could I show her what I knew was there? Something changed in her face then, softened, as if I'd really touched her. I shot away, but I wasn't just taking pictures. I was turning into film, with the shutter wide open to the light, pressing Elizabeth's hurt right into me, just as if it were my hurt too.

When I printed up the film and showed it to her, she wept. And here she was, so beautiful, everything right about her life. Except she felt bad about this hole inside her where a kid should be, and worse, about my seeing it.

Yet she liked my taking her picture, as if I were a fortune-teller who could see her in my crystal ball and tell her most times how strong and beautiful she was. If I felt something going on inside her, she'd have me take her photo, being slow with words as I was. Only now she'd sit in front of my camera, a look in her eyes like a sheer curtain drawn over a window, her smile saying come on Bonnie, guess what's on my mind. So I had the shutter clicking as if I were a tourist and she was the Taj Mahal, and Elizabeth just kept on looking at me, kind of amused. Once she told me with a faraway smile that she liked me best the way I was when I took pictures, a great silence except for the eyes.

So I got to feeling this was the way I should be, quiet inside, like a kid who didn't know how to talk yet.

She always had lots of words because she wrote for the *Star*, mostly about people in trouble, broken families, runaway kids, and battered women. She helped me sell my photos there, and that's how I got in with her friends, though I was nowhere near as smart as they were; the light I saw inside them made my eyes hurt sometimes. There was Gordon, kind of icy blond and good-looking, a Greenpeace bumper sticker on the back seat of his ten-speed; he was very intense, always talking politics. And the guy I married, Allan, who worked at the *Star* with Elizabeth: long brown hair, dark eyes a little sad behind his wire-rimmed glasses, as if he could see his own death barrelling towards him in a stupid crackup on the 401, but that was still years away; I couldn't see it inside him then.

We were all real close to each other, like beads on a string; Elizabeth strung us together, but we weren't beads, we were humans and, because we were human, the string broke. Maybe it snapped when Allan died, sent us all rolling downhill; maybe the whole thing started to shred years ago, I don't know. Once I lost Allan, I didn't care what happened; it got so bad that one night, when Elizabeth was away, I went into Gordon's room and put my arms around him and asked him to hold me. He kissed my hair, so that I could feel him breathing in my loneliness, as if it was a scent. I missed Allan so terribly, I pretended Gord was him, that's all; trouble was, if Gord had wanted to sleep with me, I probably would have done that, too. That was the worst part of being out of it, knowing the harm you could do and not caring.

And soon after that, Elizabeth and Gordon left for

a plot of land in B.C. They'd had it with Toronto and burnout and the summer air thick as soup; they wanted to make new friends, that's what Elizabeth told me. Her eyes nailed mine when she said it. I figured my camera had gone and touched the empty part of her once too often; somehow it was my fault she'd found out she was human: beautiful except for that one missing piece. Maybe it was too much for her to feel me carrying Allan's death like a stillborn baby in my gut. Maybe just the look of me scared her, as if this time she was the one with the camera and she saw in my face her own death coming. Elizabeth, so poised and beautiful, and here I was unravelling her the way moths eat holes into fine wool. Anyway, after they left, they wrote for a while, and I wrote back, and then their letters stopped, just as if I'd said or written something wrong.

Finally it hits me, what I have to do to get an answer. Forget writing; what if I set out to show her how bad I feel that a friend of mine would treat me like that? Why don't I just do a photo exhibit; I could call it *Missing Persons*; it would be about all the people who disappear on this earth every day. Good night, she'd probably hear it reviewed on the CBC. I could send them the catalogue; Elizabeth and Gordon in a photo-montage, right alongside the missing women of Argentina and the kids who never came home from Tienanmen Square. Elizabeth loves seeing pictures of herself; she'll call for sure.

So after six months of being out of it, I get myself cleaned up, put on some decent clothes, and go to one of my favourite galleries on Queen Street to talk up my idea. They love it, only they ask me what the hell planet I'd disappeared to, talk about going missing.

Back in my darkroom, I start to enlarge what I want to print. Limbs, parts of bodies, first one of Elizabeth's eyes, then her mouth, but as I do this, everything starts to change from the inside out, as if the look in the eye and the odd smile are finally going to give up their secrets. The deep blue of the iris gets bigger and bigger till the pupil spills right out of it like an oil slick into the ocean; the mouth goes from soft and amused to an angry ripple. Suddenly I realize all this is coming from inside of me, like a torrent; now I'm going after Elizabeth with the only weapon I have, taking all those noses, eyes, fingers, limbs, making them bloated and ugly as they float in the bath like they're drowning there, and then I pull them out of the tray and clip them up on the line to dry, hanging up chunks of Elizabeth. That's when I finally see it so clearly my eyes almost hurt. I've been lying to myself; it wasn't just love I felt for her. I wanted to see her one more time so I could spit the words out: you hurt me, Elizabeth, I let you shut me up, and now I can hardly find words to touch another human being, not even my own kid; me spending half my life tugging at your sleeve like a deaf-mute; saying here, Elizabeth, look at a goddamn picture of how fucking bad it hurts that you buggered off, please look.

So there I am crying, shit on this; everything a blur in front of my eyes in the dark, and the darker and more blurry it gets, the more I see, all the people I loved and the pictures I made out of them. That's when I start to think I'll have to do what a kid does, putting pictures into words, telling them to people, writing them down, which is what I'm doing now.

Tired and sad, I leave the darkroom and walk out into my studio, where the walls are covered with old photographs. It's a whole world I made up, all gone now; I run my fingers over them tenderly, over hair and eyes and arms and legs and faces, what I once brought to life in my friends. I press my face against the wall, my arms and legs too, as if the wall of people could reach out to hold me. I feel tears sting my face like acid; wonder what, if anything, I have learned.

*

The *Missing Persons* exhibit is a big success; they're letting it run for six weeks and after all the critics and the artsy types go through, you should see the people who are starting to show up; a white-haired lady who lost her family in Auschwitz, a bunch of parents trying to find street kids, two Jamaican brothers, their folks gone in a hurricane; they all have stories they want to tell me. So I feel part of a circle of people who've all lost someone; part of this broken circle called the human race.

A few weeks after the opening, I'm home around suppertime and I hear a key in the lock. Celine, she likes startling me; here she comes clunking in, flings open the door without any hello. This always makes me nervous, and without even thinking, I hunt around for a cigarette. While I'm doing this, she takes the nylon sack she has slung over her shoulder, opens it up, and dumps the stuff inside it all over the floor. Letters spill out, at least fifty of them; some of the stamps are foreign.

"Your fan mail," she shrugs. "I went to see your show. The gallery lady asked me to drop it off."

I nod very slowly, try to imagine that dented mailbox in the front hall bulging with all these letters;

remember myself in jeans and ratty slippers trudging downstairs every morning, just hoping. Celine has her eyes on me and now she's smiling a little, a small, wry, hesitant smile. She's reading my mind, I can tell.

"What the fuck, enjoy your mail," she remarks.

She looks a little sad as she says this. And now I just wish I could hold her in my arms, tell her I'm so sorry for neglecting her, for all my time fretting over Elizabeth while she stomped around noisy with hurt. A memory shivers through me of a mine disaster long ago. I still hear those rocks falling; but this time it's as if Celine is at the bottom of the mine. I love her, I'm scared she'll disappear, but how do I tell her that; we're too damn much alike, we still find it hard to say we need each other.

I'm so caught up in thinking that I let the unlit cigarette fall from my mouth. Celine bends down, picks it up, and hands it to me. Then very slowly she takes the matches from the table, strikes one, waits for the flame to dance on the tip of the match, then lights my cigarette. I thank her, and she says no problem. Something in me wants to grab a camera, hold this moment, the beauty of her young face, solemn in the glow of the flame, but I don't do it, I can't.

Celine nods slowly, as if she understands. Then she gets up and leaves, closing the door behind her, the thunk of her boots on the stairway fading away in the dark.

BEIRUT GARDEN

There it was, just as I had seen it in my dream, not what you'd call a fancy dress-up place; there was a good feeling to it, that they'd serve a meal to an out-of-towner in jeans and nobody'd mind. This was exactly what I'd expected, right down to the white-gabled roof on the old house, spotless windows half open, bouncing the sun off the glass, that's how clean they were. Even the curtains, I dreamt those, too; an Indian-cotton floral print, drifting back and forth in the April breeze. That was the upstairs part above the restaurant; the paint on the building all cracked and weathered, the dried-blood colour of an old barn, like the one Bill and I never got around to fixing up, and the thought of that made me sad. Still, this was a good enough place, a safe-looking neighbourhood for a big city like Toronto; Cabbagetown was kind of a homey name, I told Bill that, and he threw back his head and laughed, his blue eyes crinkled up and full of mischief, the first time in weeks I'd seen him happy.

"Marie, you check this sign?" he asked. He yanked off his cap with the John Deere tractor on it, his hair the colour of dust on the road, soft brown.

I looked a little closer. PRIDE OF BEIRUT CAFÉ was what it said.

"Beirut restaurant and drive-in morgue," Bill drawled.

I was only half listening, I was reading another sign, a small handwritten one alongside the door, ROOM FOR RENT, GARDEN KNOWLEDGE HELPFUL. Nudging Bill, I got him to look.

"What did I tell you, this is it," I said very softly.

"Home sweet home," Bill whispered, letting his lips brush the top of my hair. Home used to mean Niagara, our farm near Vineland south of the Queen E, but it was gone, which I'm sure was why my mind started wandering in my sleep to this room with a gabled roof over a Lebanese restaurant; where the hell else in T.O. could we afford to live, Bill had work but he wouldn't take charity, not even staying at his buddy's place. Sometimes I got lucky seeing things in dreams, maybe I found us a room for a few weeks, low rent for mowing the grass, touch wood. So we opened the door and went inside, heard a bell jingle and bang against the glass.

The café was all white, very sunny, full of green plants so you almost felt you were outside; there was a big window and a tilted skylight that let the sun in, hard and bright, like the glint of a diamond. This isn't T.O., I thought, this is the kind of light you get in the country, white against the shingles of the house at noontime, white that hurts your eyes, only this is another country, full of oriental rugs and long-necked brass pots and a big framed poster of a stucco city, a quiet harbour by the sea, and the word in French, *Liban*; the twang and wail of music you can tap your foot to, only the music's like crying.

Just as I was thinking this, the maître d' came over and asked if he could help. He looked at us kindly, but what a strong face: dark, as if a cloud were drifting over the light in it. Dark eyes, too; a curved nose, full lips, and a moustache, wiry black hair just starting to go grey. There was something very dignified and proud about the look of him: smart clothes, a white and blue pinstriped shirt, navy trousers, and a lot of gold: gold ring, gold watch, and around his neck a small gold cross on a chain. As he showed us to a table, he told us his name was Youssouf, we could call him Joe, he was the owner of the café.

"You don't understand something, ask, please," he said, glancing at the menus.

He figured right, we didn't understand anything, and when he came back to take our order, we let Joe tell us what was good. As he did so, he kept looking at me, his eyes dark and very serious, not like a man with an eye for a pretty face, more like he recognized me from somewhere. I figured he thought I was Lebanese because I'm just as dark, but I'm not, I'm Italian and French, lots of Lebanese people speak French, so he was close. Anyway, you could tell Joe was seeing me in little bits, shiny black hair feathered and cut short; large brown eyes, small face, small woman; he was looking a little worried, as if the parts of my body belonged to one of those awful jigsaw puzzles with nine hundred pieces and he was missing one. He stroked his moustache, looking thoughtful as he did.

"You want to rent my room, you have trouble finding a place, yes?" Joe asked. Bill looked stunned.

"How'd you know that?" he asked him.

"Five days the sign is on the door and no one comes

in with baggage," Joe replied. "Just you."

After lunch, he took us up the back stairs to see the furnished room next to his apartment. That was when it started, I guess, the first time I saw something of the place Joe came from, as I stepped into that clean room with pale yellow walls and a threadbare Persian carpet on the floor, the walls full of brass trays and travel posters of Greek and Roman ruins. The room felt alive, as if it were a mind lit up with thoughts and memories, the mind of someone whose hands polished the old pot-bellied brass lantern hanging by chains from the ceiling, cleaned its lacy metalwork and coloured stained-glass windows; the whole room and everything in it stirred and moved with life. As I stared at the lantern, I watched it flickering in the shadows as if it were night, I saw dim faces in the candle through the glass, it was hanging in the arched white doorway of an old stucco building leading into a garden, and I felt sure then that it carried something of Joe's life; maybe he found the lantern in the tower of a church in a Mediterranean harbour, where it guided sailors home, long ago. What a picture, I was dreaming wide awake, that's all; seeing more, much more, than I could understand just then.

While I was feeling all this, Bill told Joe we'd take the room, now what was this about gardening, the note on the sign outside. Joe said we'd talk more about it, then he invited us for coffee later that evening.

"So you are real farmers," he said, and he smiled, as if it were an honour having us as tenants. What's a farmer with no land, we didn't feel like farmers any more, we felt like a pair of failures. I wish Joe hadn't reminded us, even if he was trying to be kind.

For sure Bill felt that way too; as soon as Joe left, he sat down on the bed, didn't say anything, just slumped forward, his face in his hands. Something in him looked defeated, I could just hear him thinking, forty and flat broke, stuck doing car tuneups in T.O. for the rest of my life. The same way he looked the day the bank called the loan that finished off the farm, fists clenched, knuckles white, only then I put my hands around his, rubbing them warm, as if they were frozen stuck. Finally he relaxed, opened his hands, let me rub his fingers one by one, until the feeling of all the hard work in them went running through his veins, the hopes and memories of a whole life stuffed in some banker's pocket, and he turned away, his face in his hands and wept, that was how bad he felt.

So here in the room I sat with my arm around him, and Bill pulled his hands from his face, clasped them together, and whispered, it's done now, isn't it, meaning our life on the farm, and I nodded, yes, Bill, it's done. And I shut my eyes and saw us lying in the big pine bed in the upstairs room of the old brick-and-gabled farmhouse where generations of Bill's family slept and gave birth, and I saw the apple orchards, the rows of carefully tended vines, and all that was familiar drifting into the shadows, and I nodded, yes, Bill, it's done.

*

Joe told us he always kept the TV on in his apartment, it was good company, a friendly eye, but when visitors came he turned the sound off. He also smoked French cigarettes from an ornate brass box which he placed on a tray full of honey pastries and tiny cups of black, sweet coffee. As we talked, Joe asked a lot of questions about why we were here, but he was very tactful and kind about our losing the farm; neighbourly, not the kind of landlord we expected in Toronto. Eventually, he got around to telling us his plan to grow tomatoes, herbs, and fresh salad greens, and to hire us as his gardeners; later there would be a veranda out back so his customers could eat with the scent of mint and lemon basil, patio dining in the Beirut Garden, good idea, yes? Joe looked right at us as he spoke.

"You still would like to farm, I cannot give that," he said. "You try this instead, why not?"

He gestured, his arms outstretched, as if he could hand us comfort. Bill nodded, very slowly.

"No reason not to," he said.

Joe looked so pleased, he offered Bill another smoke and patted him on the back as if they were old buddies. Then he warmed up my coffee and invited us to relax and watch TV.

We caught the end of the baseball game, then the news, an oil spill, dying gulls, really depressing; something on taxes which made Bill swear; a women's march on Parliament Hill, a bomb going off in one of these nameless places where bombs are forever going off, a man in fatigues all caked in blood, I didn't need this.

Neither did Joe, because the screen went black.

"I'm sorry," he said. "I will not look." For a moment Joe sat with his head bowed, hands clasped around the channel-changer. Then he raised his eyes. "Respect," he whispered. "When people from my country die, I turn off the TV, out of respect. A moment of silence. Otherwise, the bodies pile up too fast, one bad news on top of the next."

"I understand," I said.

Joe shook his head adamantly, staring at the dark screen all the while. "No, you do not," he answered. "It is not your fault you do not."

Bill and I figured we should leave. The two of us said goodnight to Joe, leaving him in front of the TV, his hands folded, head bowed before the black screen, black for the dead.

*

I wondered what I could do to let Joe know we understood. For sure he'd lost someone back home, but he was too proud to talk about it and I wasn't one to pry. On the other hand, I wasn't one to leave people alone at a time like that, either. At least in the country, when a neighbour died, we knew exactly what to do: we'd bring over casseroles and soups and pies for the family and the people who came to pay their respects. They all did whatever they could to help; there was the year Bill's cousin died at planting time, and the neighbours seeded his hundred acres of winter wheat so the family would have a crop. All these kindnesses, like snapshots in an album you carry all your life, the faces of decent people, the things they do to comfort the living; I found it so hard to imagine how anyone could get on without them. I wasn't naïve, though, I read a lot, I knew about Lebanon from the TV news, you feel a sadness there you can't even begin to touch, like the hurt you get in your throat when tears won't come. Maybe there wasn't any comfort for the likes of Joe, I hated to think that.

In the meantime I felt I needed a little comfort

myself, so I was happy to dig and hoe and plant; the gardening would be my job since Bill was working days. I rented a small garden tractor and dug up the narrow strip of land behind the restaurant, right up to an old wooden fence that faced the rear of a laundromat. Once the soil was loose, I scooped it up in my hands, sniffed the rich brown warmth of it, crumbled the earth with my fingers as if I were digging up all I'd buried in memory, the vines of Niagara heavy with fine grapes, Gamay Noir, Maréchal Foch, Pinot Chardonnay; I shut my eyes and felt the rumble of the tractor in the seat of my pants and the sun like honey on my skin, remembered the taste of ripe peaches, which are summer to the mouth; thought of our son, who'll never have a chance to know this life, good as it was; he's off at college studying computers, he'll never farm.

Then I shrugged it all off and kept working, telling myself things never stay the same as you remember them, farming couldn't have been all that good or you wouldn't have gone broke doing it. It made me think of Bill when he used to show me the stars at night and tell me their names, saying they were so far away, it took the light a hundred thousand years to reach your eye, and by then a star could have exploded or collapsed or turned into a lump of cold porridge in the mind of God for all you know; for sure memory tricks you, I told myself, just like that light.

Joe must have sensed I was thinking all this, I'm sure he did, especially the day the truck came with peat and topsoil for the garden and he offered to help me unload the bales. He looked at me kindly; maybe he realized he was standing on a small patch of memory, the farm laneway,

Bill and my son pulling up in the truck, the engine humming.

"You are missing home today?" he asked me.

I nodded; Joe must have known what that was like.

"I bet you must miss your folks sometimes," I said.

Joe lit a cigarette, took a deep drag, let it out slowly. His face looked troubled, he didn't seem in a hurry to talk.

"I miss nobody," he finally answered. "The sunlight I miss. What grows outside, olive trees, fresh figs, that I miss."

Joe had had a big garden next to his restaurant in Lebanon, he told me that much. A life's work to make such a thing, he would not garden again now; those were his words.

He ground out his cigarette and got back to work, he wasn't going to say more. All that was left of his old life hung invisible in the air, its lingering scent around me as I slit open the bales and ploughed the soil and peat into the beds. As I worked, I could feel his world opening in my mind like a ripe fruit, I could see into his orchard, where the fruit yielded easily to the hand, where there were faces, moving patterns of the light through shadows, and I understood that this was my work, why I was here: I was planting the garden Joe had never left.

*

As time passed, Bill and I both tried to make the best of things, getting used to the neighbourhood just south of Carlton Street, planting and seeding and hoeing together on weekends. My mind would still slip away, less and less back to the farm, more often into some other daydream that made no sense, so I began pretending that in a city with so many quiet people, the air had to be full of ghosts and visions and imaginary places, and I was just a big antenna pulling in other people's dreams. That was how it was the day we were hoeing rows for lettuce seed when I stopped what I was doing, my eyes drawing me towards the brick wall as if it were a face.

Someone was watching me, I was sure; slowly I turned myself around in a circle, gripping the hoe with both hands, swinging like the needle of a compass towards the brick wall and the row of new metal garbage cans we had placed by the kitchen door. Bill could tell something was wrong, he came over and put his arm around me. You were looking at somebody, he whispered, no one here but us, hon, and he leaned over and kissed my cheek. It was gone then, whatever it was, and I went back to work, but I felt uneasy.

An hour later, Joe came out to the garden and told us how happy he was with our work, and that put me at ease, so I let him know what had happened.

"Maybe you've got a ghost out here." I smiled, pointing in the direction of the garbage cans.

For a minute Joe didn't answer, just shook his head slowly.

"I don't believe," he said, looking away. "Not in ghosts."

Nothing wrong with ghosts, we had ghosts at the farm all the time, I told him that, but Joe said when people die, they just go, there are no such things.

Then when I took a break, I noticed Joe, still in the garden, picking a few flowers. He was watching, listening. All you could hear were the birds, a soft wind in the trees, the rumble of cars on the road, like faraway thunder.

*

I worked in the garden for the rest of the day, and I found myself feeling spooked any time I was hoeing near the brick wall behind the restaurant. And then that night I had this dream, the worst kind of dream, not because it scared me, but because it was happening right in the room where I slept, right outside and downstairs, so when I woke up and told it to Bill, I wasn't really sure if I had dreamt it or seen it happen.

There I was, lying in bed in the dark, somewhere between awake and asleep, when I heard noises out in the back yard, clatter and bang, just as if someone had pulled a lid off one of the garbage cans and dropped it on the concrete. Then everything got real quiet in my sleep, a sound that was almost black, then there was another metallic sound, but softer, a scraping noise, somebody trying to be quiet, opening and closing the shed where we kept the hoes and clippers and work gloves. For sure it was a woman, you could hear her voice coming from the back yard, small and very clear, and then a man's voice answering hers, I was sure I heard him say the name Renée, and then the voices began to fade, until the only sound I could hear was the clock on the bedside table, ticking too loud.

I got out of bed and went to the window, and Bill did too, because by now all the noises had woken him up. Then I stared down, oh Jesus, did I stare.

The garden was lit up, the leaves were cut glass in the moonlight, the sky was tipped on edge like a great black bowl, stars falling out of it, breaking and shattering on the ground. In the middle of the garden there was a young woman wearing a straw hat and gardening gloves and jeans, she was on her knees picking berries and putting them in a basket, and there was a young man walking towards her; he was carrying a large corrugated box, he looked like he was going to help her pick, neither of them seemed to notice the lopsided tilt the sky was making with the earth, or that it was night, or that the stars were on fire, burning in the grass.

How do you think she got here? I whispered to Bill.
Likely fell out of the sky, she'll go back, he answered.
"No, she can't, Bill," I said out loud.
"Why not?"
I paused, the words stuck on my lips.
"Because she's dead." Those were the words.

I said the words out loud, saw everything slow down, fear and terror crossing this woman's face in a slow dance, the basket slipping out of her hands, being pulled towards the sky along with her body, arms and legs spread wide; slowly she began floating upward, hat off, braids flying, mouth in a silent black O that grew larger and larger, until it swallowed her and the garden in darkness and all the light from the stars on the grass went out.

There was a terrible flash, an explosion, screams besides my own, arms and legs dismembered, blood in a soft drizzle falling to the earth; I heard the TV going dead, Joe's TV, and I woke up then.

*

For sure it was a dream about the end of the world Joe knew. And after I woke Bill up with my crying, I wrote down the whole dream and the name of the young woman, Renée, young enough to be Joe's daughter. Wife, kids, friends; poor Joe, maybe everyone he loved back home was dead in the fighting. He missed only the weather in Lebanon, he told me once.

*

We became friends with Joe, and gradually he began to give up his silence about who and what he had lost. Or maybe he could sense that I had lived inside his garden and so I already knew.

"You see I leave home and come to Toronto," Joe said to us. "Just like you I come, with nothing."

Night after night he talked to us like this, until the words fell from his lips and broke with the weight of suffering they carried. Then he poured us coffee and passed around his cigarettes and none of us spoke, because the room was heavy with memory like the air before thunder: stucco buildings resting in the shelter of a harbour town, white with sun as if the city were a star, only the light travelling from this star began its journey years ago; the star is on fire, burning in the grass.

HARD NEWS

Jeff chases stories, he's an urban hunter in a black fringed leather jacket, he dresses all in black, as if he were in mourning. Lean and intent, he hunches over a radio tape and edits, a deft flick of the blade prying loose all hesitations and catches in the voice; he is skinning thought to the bare bone. This small, precise ritual is the end of the daily chase for hard news: important stories, calamities. Jeff does not do soft news, or "sofnus", as they slug it on the wire, events judged to be trivial because they don't kill people or otherwise upset their daily routine; that's my department.

Today you can almost smell hard news on Jeff, hard-breathing news as he slices into his tape, then bounds over to the computer screen, words clicking out of his fingers. All week he has been working on a series, reciting a mantra of planetary death: drought in the Sahel, global warming, the sun like an angry fist punching its way through the hole in the ozone. Now they're sending him off to cover a fire and train derailment in the west end, a chemical spill. War used to be this kind of proving-ground for young men; Jeff is armed with recording gear as he strides out the door.

Only he's afraid; he told me he's scared of poisons, swigs bottled water, and lives on greens; he is becoming gaunt, too thin. I worry about Jeff, I follow the chemical spill on the TV monitor; four people have already lost their lives in a fire they can't put out. The skeleton of a tanker-car is lying on an embankment, charred and gutted like a carcass picked of its flesh.

Jeff returns later, pale and subdued. He tells me he saw two people dying of some acid that burns skin to the bone. Convinced he's in shock, I offer him half a sandwich; something to eat would make him feel better; but he says no, he really couldn't eat.

Sitting down, he threads the reel of tape onto the editing machine, wriggles out of his leather jacket, hunts for a chalk marker and a razor blade, puts on a headset, but on second thought removes it. In this way I can hear what he has salvaged from the wreck, the disembodied voice of a police officer threading its way through a crackling of flame, we don't know the number of dead, sir.

Jeff is listening with his whole body. Tape begins to slither to the floor in a brown heap; it folds and ripples over the leather jacket he's peeled off like the rind of a fruit. Now he is ankle-deep in tape, in voices, sirens, and the hiss of flame. Not cutting any more, not even listening, Jeff lets all the tape spin off the reel and onto the floor, as if he were skinning flesh to the bare bone, because he is a reporter and this is what he saw.

WHAT HISTORY TEACHES

The gun is a way of looking into things, her dad told her; not violence but a discipline, a focus for the eyes and mind. It was the most advice he'd ever given, the strangest she'd ever received. Chris, her dad, had been a sharpshooter once. Her name was his idea: Lucii with two i's, one for each of the organs of seeing.

A different kind of light, the flash from a gun, more precisely a rifle, a .22, his, the old worn stock bent to the curve of her shoulder. Sixteen years of life stacked up inside her like a cord of firewood in the shed behind her family's house in Timmins, Ontario, dry tinder, ready for the match. Her dad, flannel-jacketed, cigarette bobbing up and down between his bearded lips, the embers glowing like the signal lights of bush planes trying their damnedest to land in the dark.

"A gun has no brain, Lucii. It sees what you see. It shoots what you shoot. Thinking counts."

"I'll do my best."

"You'll do more than your best. Better than best."

Lucii looked at him. "Open season on tin cans."

"And that's all you're getting, gal."

Everyone in Timmins hunted, Lucii knew this. She asked her dad why he didn't.

"Don't think much of it" was all he said.

He'd spoken to her many times this way, his soft, drawn-out tone of voice unlike that of anyone who'd grown up near Timmins. As a child, she'd wondered how he knew all he knew about rifles and cloud formations and animal husbandry and the tending of what few crops grew here, but when she asked, he shook his head and said, just from my folks, hon, is all.

She'd never met his people, her relatives from Virginia; from the States. Some farming in his family, a lot of restlessness, her New England mother'd told her once. All the men had been in the army at one time or another, including her dad. Only he became an outlaw and deserted, ran away to Canada, her with him; it was in summer, both of them shivering in tie-dyed tops and jeans, and her mother, Alison, for one, not prepared for the chill of evenings, the grave serenity of spruce and jackpine, the hard-rock shield set firm as a stubborn jaw. They were headed way north, like pioneers, leaving a country that'd got itself up to no good, landing at a friend's place in Timmins, starting their lives all over. Their families had no use for them, called them traitors, running off the way they did.

This was their history, at least the one they told her.

*

Lucii trusts Chris and Alison; after all, they're her parents. Her birth lies within the story they tell, as if the story itself were her mother. What would it mean for her sanity if they were lying?

Indeed.

For now, let's grant the two of them partial truth and good intentions. Lucii's father must have wanted her to see much, bestowing insight and depth of vision in the peculiar spelling of her name. Whether or not her mother shared this wish, we know that at least one parent wanted the child to be a witness, to seek the truth beyond appearances. Perhaps they had nothing to hide after all.

Yet it's also possible that Lucii's seeing-name was a curse, that her parents needed to implant in her psyche secrets that would spring to virulent life, consuming her in the same way that cancer cells devour healthy tissue. Maybe this is how her parents survived, by casting devils out of their bodies, into a child's. This is the curse of the evil Other, the plague of history, what humans carry as dogs carry fleas.

Lucii's mother had a favourite aphorism:

"Let me recite what history teaches," said Gertrude Stein. "History teaches."

*

Mental Notes (overheard by Lucii, age sixteen):

"She's too caught up with rifles," said her mother. Her dad laughed.

"Like we were."

"I still don't approve."

"She's using blanks, babe. Not givin' the man what-for."

"Drop it, Chris."

"Why? That bastard asked for what he got. His bank was funding the war."

"Right now we're talking about Lucii."

"Shooting'll fix her tired eye. Relax."

Her mother crying, it's 'cause of what we did she got it in the first place.

Her father's voice, soft now: come on hon, it couldn't be. Just isn't true, babe. Just isn't.

*

Lucii complained to her friends that her mother and dad were hippies, back-to-the-landers, out of date. They had an old black-and-white TV in her house, and no cable; they ate granola, beansprouts, and wholewheat bread; her dad did carpentry and home repairs and her mom wore Refuse the Cruise buttons all over her granny dress, only shit, Lucii thought, it was 1983 and her parents were stuck inside the past like two dead flies in amber. Only she knew it was more than the hokey stuff that got to her, her mother's prayers at dinner for polluters and warmakers, and her trying to look reverent and wanting to squirm, half wondering if girls could join the army, and how old you had to be. It was what she saw in unguarded moments, the lake-blue darkness in her father's wary eyes. No emotion in her mother's face, but something worse in it to frighten her: an unreadable code of lines and facial depressions, like the imprint of fossils in calcified rock.

Lucii knew there had been trouble once, that this was the reason why her parents had fled. Yet she couldn't ask them what they'd done, fearing she'd lose them, as if the authorities might hone in on her voice the way instruments pick up seismic rumbles underground. Dumb as her father's rabbits when it came to this: eyes, ears and nose alert, learning to watch, to listen.

*

Memory (Lucii, age eight):
She wakes up to the sweet, burning smell of hash, the sound of them in bed through cracker-thin walls, her father's voice, then her mother's. The sound a fawn makes jammed in a leg-hold trap, her crying.
"What's eatin' you, babe?"
"I feel them in the room, that man'n' woman."
"Tell 'em to fuck off."
"I can't. They're on my conscience." Stillness, then cunning in his voice as it coiled and tightened around her.
"You got conscience 'bout as much as I do."
"Shove it, Chris." He doesn't. His voice is cajoling now.
"'New York City banker'n' his rich-bitch wife, human shit,' you called 'em. 'Old Warbucks, offed and crappin' his guts.' You were so hot you coulda fucked right there. Conscience, my ass."
"I'm not like that now. I'm going home."
"You go south, you're fried, babe. You want that?"
Her mother crying, like maybe the answer was yes.

*

Her mother wore her hair in plaits soft and homespun as braided bread, made herself fragrant with cinnamon and

—42—

apples, a teacher of very young children.

At Christmastime she'd taken to bringing a large box to school so the little kids could dump in warplanes, toy soldiers, guns, klunk-klunk, thank you, boys and girls (but mostly boys), I'll sell it for scrap and give the money to charity. The year Lucii was fourteen, Ronald Reagan was enraging her mother; an armed and dangerous man, she called him. That was why she took the full box home, found a hammer, then found Lucii.

"I want you to trash them with me," she said, pointing to the toys. "Symbolic acts have the power to change us."

"Heavy, Mom."

"The arms race is heavy, Lucii. You could be dead in a decade."

"Lighten up, jeez."

"Lucii, this is important."

"Mom, this is looney-tunes."

Lucii stomped out of the room, heard behind her the banging and smashing of a hammer, the wild staccato of her mother's frenzy as if she were a prisoner desperate to escape, flying apart with the bits of tank turrets, rotors, gun barrels, everything breaking.

*

Her mother, afraid of Lucii's wandering eye, aesthetically offensive, motor-scooter quick, snooping and seeing more, not less; this and more she'd told her husband. It was an ill omen, she'd said; punishment, a broken window to the basement of the soul, a place Lucii imagined to be dark and full of cobwebs, strewn with jagged glass, wires, explosives;

her parents' secrets littering the floor like oily rags. In time there would be a fire, a conflagration.

*

"Didn't you'n' Dad ever shoot together?" Lucii was sixteen. Her mother looked as cool as March.

"Dad did. It's more a male thing."

"Is that why you don't want me doing it?"

"That and what you did to the rabbit."

"Six years ago. I felt like shit. I'm not a butcher, Mom." Her mother paled, took a deep, impatient breath.

"I want to make sure you won't become one."

"Why, does it run in families?"

"What are you talking about?"

"Whatever the hell you guys did. Why you beat it all the way to Timmins."

Her mother's voice, becalmed like a boat in still water.

"We left because the country was falling apart, dear."

"Like the walls of this house. You can hear the mice fucking."

"Watch your language, young lady."

"Okay. I didn't catch the tune. Just the rhythm section."

Her mother's eyes flashed a warning like a hunting cat's in darkness.

"Kindly drop it, Lucii."

"Then quit bugging me about the rabbit, okay?"

Her mother never pestered her again. Nights afterward were quiet, still as an animal's breathing.

*

How it was the rabbit died:

Lucii was ten years old. From her parents' room, the sweet whiff of pot, a small crazy laugh that shattered, as if her dad were a window and someone had thrown a rock through him. Silence, then her parents starting in. Her mother saying fuck me good. Bodies thudding against the bed like fists.

It was the laughter woke her up. Still groggy, Lucii pounded on the wall and the noise stopped. A few minutes later, her father came into her room and sat on her bed. He clamped his massive hands on her shoulders.

"You don't do that again." Ice chips where his eyes should be. Lucii was too frightened to cry out. His hands were clamps about to crush her bones.

"You don't go buttin' in on us, all right?"

She nodded. Her body white with pain.

"That hurt?"

Lucii wept.

"Good," he said. As if he'd opened a stuck tap, bled a rad. He let go of her, then left.

Upset and scared, Lucii took her pillow and blankets out to the shed and slept in the straw. The next morning, the creaking door woke her up. She heard her mother's careful step, then her skirts, a swishing, bird-feather sound. You'd think she'd planned it, Lucii thought. Coming in with a wake-up song.

"What are you doing out here?" her mother asked. Lucii glared at her.

"The people next door make too much noise."

"You must have been having bad dreams."

"Dad pretty near broke my bones. Guess that was a bad dream too."

Lucii told her mother what had happened, then watched her face harden, its lines like the cuts of miners' picks in rock.

"I sent him in," she said.

As punishment for the night before, Lucii had to clean the rabbits, and they stank of shit and piss and the reek of animal odour from fucking their little lives away. She opened the cage door and yanked one out.

"You fuck too much, you're dirty, and you smell," she said to the rabbit.

Her mother's voice in her head: I sent him in.

Her dad's: That hurt, Lucii? Good.

The two of them: We fuck, you listen.

It's all I do is listen to your crap, said the bone and muscle of her hands to the rabbit's body, which was not the rabbit at all, but the object of a fury she couldn't stop. Her body was plugged into a power source of rage, her hands grabbing the rabbit, squeezing it hard, slamming it against the concrete walk as if it were a fist she was ramming into walls, as if it were a letting go of the secrets of fugitives, of all that had passed through her body's memory, all the strangulated crying and screaming of ten knotted years of life, until she came to her senses and saw the rabbit's white head lying in the small yellow pool of vomit that was spreading like the yolk of an egg cracked open. Then she saw that the rabbit didn't move, and she knelt down beside it and wept.

Her parents, hearing the commotion, came running. They asked her why she'd done this. She couldn't talk, her eyes on the ground.

"It didn't want to live," was all she said.

Her father's eyes wore a glaze of fear and shame. He couldn't bear to look at her, to see the brittle face of her despair.

Lucii's mother made her wash the rabbit, wrap it in cloth, dig a hole, and bury it. She remembered crying as she did this, remembered how her parents sat in fearful silence, observing her remorse and anguish as they might observe the rain. Lucii felt she shouldn't be alive, felt the rabbit's death etched into her hands like fingerprints.

*

Whose hands? Whose fingerprints? After this, Lucii dreams her mother, the front of her dress soaked in blood, the bleeding carcasses of rabbits at her feet. Her father is there with a high-powered rifle, laughing. Again and again Lucii dreams this moment, this understanding, eternal, unfolding in her hands. Premonition or history, one or both, a dream that has drifted loose from the moorings of time, a clock with missing hands, a calendar of no days, no years.

*

Lucii, sixteen years old, tall and brush-cut boyish, leather-jacketed, studs on her ears like heads of nails. She had become gentle with rabbits; felt as she cared for them her father's eyes on her, his grave yet understanding look, as if he knew he could only watch her from a distance, through the invisible glass he had set between them.

"You should pray for the dead rabbit," said her

mother. Six years after the poor thing died, the words trickling down from her lips like blood from a gash, as if the creature were still dying. Lucii thought, Flake City, until she looked at her face, unaccountably troubled, broken as a rock cleft, a fault in the earth. She prayed for her mother.

Lucii wondered about the woman's sanity, trying not to laugh when Alison would pray at dinner for her straying eye, along with the errant souls of uranium miners and the drifting consciences of people who tested cruise missiles. She began to imagine herself as one of those ugly flying contraptions, stubby-winged as a pelican, guided by her zigzag vision, now left, now right, now over the hills. Slowpoky flying, an aerial tortoise in a world of hares. Cruising Lucii, armed and seeing everything.

*

Shooting practice: Lucii raised the rifle to her shoulder, took aim, and fired. A miss. She'd set the tin can jiggling, that's all.

"Again," said her dad.

She fired. The can sank into the weight of the bullet, fell.

"Yer hot."

Hit after hit.

"Yer dangerous, gal. Real trouble." Her dad was laughing.

Sharpshooter Lucii, her body bending into the shape of the rifle until she began to feel as if the hands gripping the gun were a marksman's hands. She was no longer seeing with her own drifting eyes, but with a brisk, cool pair of optical scanners, the muscles well aligned. The gun and Lucii, fine-tuned as the strings of instruments vibrating to a high, sweet note, the clear gold liquid of it moving through her body. No longer herself, inside another mind, another pair of eyes. What they saw: her dream, the front of a woman's dress soaked with blood.

You got Warbucks, she hears the woman say, and she's laughing. Where has Lucii heard this?

In your own sick mind, that's where, she thinks.

She fires again.

*

She fires into dreams, where stories begin, the whole cloth of them ripped and shredded in the spinning vortex of this century, just as the laws of physics shatter in the maw of a black hole, utter gravity from which no light escapes. Lucii dreams, sees, cannot help calling back from this century's darkness her family's history, which is part of the tormented history of the world, of its lost and missing, its unmourned dead. She has no relatives, no family records, only what her father gave her: the gun, a way of looking into things, a narrative form. Also her name, two eyes.

*

Memory (Lucii, age five):

She sees her mother thrashing through the bush behind their house, running in the direction of the road, her face lacerated with scratches from thorns and twigs, the sound of her boots as if her feet were crushing glass, not autumn leaves. Lucii takes one step, then another, scared she will lose her mother, even more afraid to venture into the woods. From the opposite direction she sees her dad trotting along like a sure-footed horse, senses he is angry, knows enough not to call to him. He grabs her mother, says where the hell do you think you're going, and she's sobbing I'm going to turn us in, I'm going home, you leave me be. He jumps her from behind, shoves his hands in her pockets, finds a pistol and a roll of bills. Like hell you are, you crazy bitch, he says, throwing her on the ground, face down, heaving his huge form on top of her so that there is no struggle, no sound underneath the thick navy hump of his overcoat, only his occasional push, her mother's sobs inside the drifting whisper of his voice, you want life in jail, babe, you got it right here.

*

Her dad had explained once in his slow, laconic way that the isolation of the bush got to her mother sometimes, the life of teaching miners' kids who only cared about Michael Jackson and Pac-man, and her being stuck with a sixties conscience in a place where nobody cared what exile had cost her; Timmins, with clapboard houses and slag heaps and snow that didn't melt till May, and pissed hunters with antlered deer thrown over the hoods of their muddied pickups. That was what was getting to her mother on days when she wept, locking the door of her room, refusing food. Real hard on her, a brainy woman in a mining town, and her not given to what you'd call an even temperament, he told Lucii that. Timmins didn't seem to bother him, it was part of living, grey like slush, hardly worth a mention.

Quit making up stories, Lucii told herself.

Quit imagining the scope, wide open like a window. In it, eyes like twin moons, staring back at her in the night-blackness.

A man's voice: Asshole, I'll tell you what I want. Wanna blow yer fucking peepers out is what I want.

A woman's: Freeze, bitch.

For sure you dreamt it. Concentrate and fire.

Whose eyes, what year is this?

*

She is afraid to ask her parents questions, to stir the nightmare slumbering in both of them. Retreating to the library, Lucii cranks through microfilm, digs into books about the United States in the era of Vietnam, reads about groups with names like the Panthers and the Weathermen, bombers and would-be assassins in her parents' country, finds no accounting of her mother and father, wonders if she even knows their real names. Even so, she is relieved. Her parents are fugitives melting into northern Canada like spring runoff into streams and gullies. Their story hidden until the river swells in flood.

*

Lucii raised the rifle, aimed at the can, let herself see raw chunks of colour sizzling, drawing from her gun an explosion that felt as if it had its beginnings deep inside her. Dead aim coming from beyond her eyes, from the place where she saw everything: her parents' hidden lives; in them, a century's worth of shadows.

Only the bullet was fired long before her birth, a tight, hard cylinder of madness. Hard times back then, her dad once said. Stories not worth telling.

"Now you line 'er up and shoot, Lucii."

She took aim, nicked the tin can, sent it tottering sideways, spinning.

"Wanna see you hit it dead centre. Only the clean shots count."

Lucii trained her rifle on the can and fired. All she heard was a raging white bang of a thought.

He never paid for what he did, that bastard. Here's one for my old man.

The can skittered, clunked off the post.

"You see real good," her dad said.

"Yes, dad," Lucii answered.

Yes.

*

Dream (Lucii, age sixteen):

Emptying a gun, he said to her mother, easy as taking a piss.

I'm still ashamed, she answered.

Shame turns you on. Give it up.

I can't, she said; there's death in my hands. They are tight around my own throat, and there is no end to this constriction, this crushing out of life, collapsing inside me to an infinite point of darkness, no light escaping. Ever.

Yer stoned, babe. C'mere.

The bullet you shot. Where did you hit him?
Lotsa bullets. Lotsa places, babe. Same as you did.
No, just one.
You fuckin' crazy.
You got his eyes. Lucii, the eyes of the dead in hers.
Look.

*

What Lucii saw: her mother's dress bloodied. Her eyes, round and terrible, a pair of broken clocks.

Lucii and her dad came home from target practice to see blood trickling from the rabbits' throats. Her father, his face grey and broken as gravel.

"It's still happening," her mother said. She was walking towards him, hands outstretched, as if she were asleep.

"Alison?" He stared at her.

"Let me show you what history teaches."

"What, babe?"

Her mother pulled a pistol from her apron pocket.
Lucii ran.

*

She fled into dreams, spent years inside the spinning vortex where stories begin, the whole cloth of them rent apart for ever. It was the times, she tells herself now, hardly knowing how to tell the time, all clocks being broken, all calendars gone. Observing the world, watching TV news, she remembers her mother and father, notices (or imagines) that snipers aim for the eyes first.

She is still running, even as you read this.

LOVE AND THE GENTLE ART OF FLYING

Terry Donohue couldn't have cared less that he'd been laid off, that his job in the aircraft factory had moved south and left him behind. Some job, testing computerized navigation for fighter planes so they wouldn't crap their load of bombs on the wrong target. Terry figured the way the world was going, anybody with half a brain could reprogram these systems to deliver hot pizza to your door in seconds. Out of a job, he could make a buck with a scheme like that, but he didn't want to think about it, or about much of anything to do with work right now.

 Over the past few months he had done more than enough thinking, and at the age of twenty-eight he had come to the conclusion that he wanted to spend the rest of his life in his one-bedroom apartment on the twenty-first floor of a Mississauga highrise, designing and building experimental model airplanes out of balsa wood, toothpicks, and paper scraps. He had no other ambitions. He didn't want to upgrade himself to Instrument Test Technician Category Fifty-Two and end up making a lateral move to some whacked-out, Bible-thumping air-force town in the States; he refused to buy a house because he liked heights, and he didn't care if he made money because he had so few ideas about how to spend it. Even buying groceries seemed like a waste of time; he stayed thin, no matter what he ate. Helen used to send out for ribs and pizza, fries and chocolate cake, but fat didn't take to him. His face was still angular and gaunt, his pale grey eyes wary and puzzled, as if he'd gotten lost and needed directions to somewhere, anywhere. In winter he let his thick blond hair grow long, hid himself in scarves, pullovers, and a battered leather jacket; summer was a nightmare of blistered skin, ozone holes, and Number Forty sunblock. Convinced the gene for survival was missing from his DNA, Terry had decided that, for the moment at least, he would add a few years to his life by hiding out.

Excuses, Helen used to tell him; he made too many excuses for himself, and she was right. The truth was he had one big mess to sort through, job or no job, and he'd decided to let his skilled hands do the sorting, with no interference from his zonked-out brain, which had already provided him with far too many excuses and distractions.

He began by picking up a strip of balsa wood, feeling the smooth, light weight of it in his hand. Right away he thought of Helen, thought of flying, put the wood aside, opened a beer and drank it down, feeling against his tongue the cool sweetness of her mouth. God, what he wouldn't give to have her back. He could see her face, slate-blue eyes the colour the sky gets just before lightning cracks it down the middle, her smile all come-and-get-it mockery and laughter; he remembered how he'd bury his face in her long hair, wanting to drown in the dark waves falling to her shoulders, how his body hurt for wanting to drown inside her.

Helen was studying to be an engineer. She wanted to design airplanes; apart from this one ambition, he realized, she had never asked for very much. She hadn't liked domestic life any more than he had, never expected him to get interested in marriage or kids or buying a house; they both swore they'd never live together. They gave each other room, letting the space between them stretch like a rubber band until it snapped and sent them flying right into each other; sex was great then, except for the near-collisions with the ancient model aircraft swinging over Terry's bed. He remembered one night when Helen's eyes scanned all the junk on the ceiling as if she'd never seen it before. She started to laugh, and Terry could feel a high-voltage crackle, the sparks in her eyes jumping the gap to his. He realized it wasn't the planes but something she saw inside him, a childish fighting instinct embarrassing enough to make him swear he'd chuck all his airborne garbage, only she threw her arms around him and kissed him on the mouth.

"C'mon, cowboy, don't you ever laugh at your-self?" she asked. She started wrestling him out of his clothes and they made love right in the middle of that flying zoo; after she left, he ripped down his battle craft as if they had nothing at all to do with him. It was a bad habit he hadn't gotten over, trashing planes like dead insects, yanking off their wings.

Two years later Helen left him. Terry was a pilot and they had gone flying the previous September, over the escarpment and bush country that coiled like the spine of a primitive reptile around the city of North Bay. There was an accident, he ditched the plane, his fault. All he ever really understood was that airborne craziness was no longer a joke for Helen; she'd had enough.

Over and over he spun the moments of calamity through his mind: turn and bank, nose down, wing down, spiral to earth like a dead leaf in a twist of smoke; it was a compulsion that protected him from the worst pangs of grief and regret. Eight months later he was still doing this, only now he sat drinking beer and sketching an unfinished wing as it started to move and lift from the drawing-board. It belonged to a very large and elegant wooden plane, to Helen's love of flying as well as his, to his need to understand why everything had fallen apart, to the memories that pushed their way through his fingers and onto the page.

*

As he sketched, Terry had to admit that nobody in his or her right mind flew anywhere in the bush outside North Bay during air-force practice runs; nobody needed the thrill of getting buzzed by a herd of thundering Rambos. He told the board of inquiry he'd never meant to do anything that stupid, swearing that when the big fighters came slicing the sky wide open like they were carving the guts right out of it, he figured the guys in the control tower must have all had heart attacks and died, because they weren't saying a whole lot to help him get out of the way. Either that, said the investigator who pulled his licence, or Terry wasn't paying attention earlier when they warned him to clear out.

As for what actually happened, Terry could only remember Helen's voice screaming at him, you're dropping too damn fast! He'd made his bank too steep, tipping the plane nose-down into a spiral, the horizon at a weird slope, the bush rushing up and ripping and tearing at the plane as it hit the trees, shards of metal flying into the trunks of spruce and flaming red maple. On the ground and barely conscious, Terry called out for someone, hearing the crackle of fire, then the sound of footsteps crunching on leaves, a big twig snapping under the weight of heavy feet: one round-toed boot, then another, a very shiny and black pair with thick heels and soles, all laced up, and over the top of the boots, baggy pants, olive green. He saw Helen on a stretcher, buried under a mound of army blankets; he could feel her cry in his throat.

*

Three months laid up in hospital; Terry remembered that, too, figuring he got more visitors than he deserved, including one or two buddies from the shop and one part-timer from the summer office crew. She was Christina Melnyk, an art student barely out of her teens. She had told Terry once that she was fascinated by an intricate model airplane he had made for her dad, who was also his boss. Terry had said he'd show her how to make them, but he figured it would be a while before he wanted to look at a plane again. He'd always thought Christina looked young, no more than sixteen; it was the way she wore her hair, old-fashioned, long and coppery, plaited in braids around her head. She had sombre green eyes and pale skin, delicate and pretty like fancy china, the kind most people try to hide from clumsy fingers or the swipe of a hand. Christina was carrying a huge black portfolio; she sat down next to Terry and asked him how he felt.

"Awful," he told her. "Fucking good for nothing."

Christina nodded and got up soundlessly, almost floating out of the chair. Then she opened her portfolio and began to tape her watercolour paintings to the bare walls, until she had covered them completely. The stark room started to feel alive, the walls breathing colour.

"Why'd you do that?" he asked her.

She looked at him kindly, her eyes perplexed, as if he should know why.

"So you wouldn't feel so bad," that was all she said before she tiptoed off. Terry sank back into the pillows, shut his eyes, felt the movement of light and colour all around him, as if they were hands resting on his body, soothing the knots of confusion and suffering there.

*

(Much later, going to bed with Helen, he remembered reaching out to touch her, his hand moving through her body as if she wasn't there; and then her turning to him, she was crying, I can't, Terry. Her trust gone, she went also, only she was naked; her injuries had made her frail as she moved from the bed out through the open window into the sky, which was in fact where he'd left her the day the plane fell. Fucking idiot he was, all the details blurred like tears into her absence, he lost her as you might lose hope, he would never remember how.)

*

His hands were thinking all this as they drew, which was

why Terry stared out the window from time to time as he sat in front of his drafting board. He was also seeing something Helen would love, not a plane but the idea of a plane, a graceful object bending to the laws of aerodynamics, its parts in delicate, perfect balance. As he looked in the distance, his eyes unfocused, imagining the smooth line of a wing spar holding a delicate latticework of ribs; his hands felt what his mind saw and he drew.

It went on for days: Terry, alone in his apartment in front of the open window, relaxing in the warm weather of early June, drafting his elegant plane, while his memories of what had happened, or what he thought had happened, moved through his fingers and onto the page, invisible as wind.

*

Terry began building the plane in the early weeks of summer. He stocked up on cold beer, thin sheets of balsa wood, cutting blades, jigs, braces, and glues; then he turned on the fans and opened his windows and the balcony door. There was space in the living room to clear, rolling up the carpet, moving what little furniture he had into the bedroom. As soon as he'd made room to work, he began cutting and sanding the parts of the plane: the fuselage, the slender ribbing of wings spread out fan-wise like an eagle's, hinges and ailerons for the trailing edges of the wings, a rudder and stabilizer for the back. Some days he looked up from his work, glanced outside, and saw the bloated and angry sun, a hot boiling eye that never shut, and he felt afraid, half convinced the heat outside might set him and his pile of wood on fire. At other times he was sure he could feel a light breeze that would lift him and his airplane into the sky as if they were as gentle and weightless as the thought of flying. Then he felt safe.

Terry needed a special kind of paper to cover all the frames, something that felt like the drifting and moving of clouds. He thought of Christina Melnyk's artwork, wondering if she could find what he needed. First he should get her to come by and have a look at the parts of his plane; she'd liked his models, she was bound to be curious. When Terry called her, she sounded hesitant and said she wasn't sure if she could make it. He figured he'd given her the wrong idea; she was just a kid and probably thought he was some kind of weirdo. Later he was surprised when she showed up clutching her black portfolio; her green eyes looked furtive and a little worried. Terry smiled at her.

"I wasn't going to come," she told him.

"I'm really building an airplane, no kidding," Terry said. Still hesitant, Christina stepped inside and looked around the living room cluttered with bits of skeletal fuselage and wings. Her smile of relief dipped and curved into a frown. "You'll never get that plane out of your apartment, Terry," she said.

"Don't want to," he told her, sure he knew what Christina was thinking; the fuselage was going to be huge, eight feet long; what the hell would he do about the wingspan, he'd have to knock out a wall. He'd already planned to assemble the plane so the nose pointed towards the balcony; that would make room for the wings, one of them poking into the alcove where normal people kept their dining-room tables. He explained all this with a shrug.

"Think of it as a new way of arranging space," he

said, but he was thinking of the space in the mind where thoughts and memories rearrange themselves as gently and aimlessly as the dust in a beam of sun.

To his surprise, Christina looked at him as if she had seen inside his mind. "A new way of flying," she said, her green eyes calm as air. Very slowly, she lifted her arms up from her sides, held them straight out from her shoulders, tossing back her coppery hair. It glistened with threads of sunlight, as if she were already moving across the sky.

*

Christina came back with paper for the wings, pale rose and yellow-orange; she also brought her sheaf of watercolours and hung them on the walls so that, even in the heat, Terry would feel the breeze coming off them. Alone during the days, he began very carefully to brace the wings and cover them with paper, and as he worked, he looked up to see the walls of his apartment move and vanish into a bright blue morning where he was floating in bed with Helen. He blinked, but this was really where he was, the sky above and below him; he was falling downward through the cloud between her legs into an oblivion he wanted and wished to Jesus would never stop, going down until he touched his own solitude like a scar from a childhood disease, one he might have prevented long before he knew her, but in the end could do nothing about. He didn't want to remember this; she was the one who'd left him, but there he was, resting in the dark space between them, tasting delicious sparks of mockery that flew off her tongue as she kissed him and teased him about the distance he kept from her. If he really wanted to bugger off, she said, she'd plunk him in a high tower and leave him there, meaning right here, which is where he was this very minute when he opened his eyes and felt himself falling helpless as rain inside the memory of her words.

Helen, where are you? he whispered out loud. He felt embarrassed, talking to the walls, naked as he peeled these memories off his skin, stretching them neatly over the wooden airframe, carefully papering them into the wings, watching the lost pieces of his life take shape as he planed the rough surfaces on the rudder and tail. Once after making love to Helen, he'd told her how his father had abandoned him and his mother for muskeg and black flies and flying cargo planes out of places like Timmins and Moosonee; eight years old, he began building model planes, looking forward to the day when he'd be a pilot, catching up with his father, who was tall and fair, who'd held him on his lap and regaled him with stories of flying, who was away for just a little while in a warm log cabin somewhere in the boreal forest.

He'd told himself one hopeful story after another, only his father never called or wrote or came back to him, or to his mother, who died not long afterwards. Finally he locked himself in his room and turned it into the cockpit of a fighter plane, where he spent hours gunning down his old man's Twin Otter, watching the bastard tumble out of the sky like a piece of shit from a seagull. Then at night he'd feel his father in the room with him, only it was his old man out for revenge. From under the covers Terry would watch the shadow of wings darting across the room, swooping and diving over the bed; hear the whistle of bullets until he could feel a pain that was not the fear of injury so much as grief. Even though his father had left him, he felt he shouldn't be as angry as he was. Sometimes he wept, wanting forgiveness.

Sick of fighting, he watched his own body turn into a shadow, thin and pale and distant. Now he was aware of a space in his life, an absence of wanting or caring much; Terry told Helen all this.

You took it out on yourself, Helen said, her voice kind.

I fucking loved him once, Terry answered. I fucking wanted to be like him, and I am.

It's not so hopeless, that was all Helen said as she put her arms around him, but then he remembered it was different the night she left, a blue curtain of suffering drawn across her eyes. You won't face what you've done, Terry, she said. You brought the plane down as if you were still chasing your old man; you could have killed us both. He'd never understood what she meant, telling him he was angry at his dad, stuck on getting even; he could still hear her voice, the words trapped like prisoners in the back of his mind: Terry, you went to war, you got so angry you knifed me with your plane, now you think I can trust you in bed as if nothing had happened; don't you realize I can't?

He let the memory of her words run free, the truth Helen spoke when she left.

*

Days melted in the heat while Terry watched his flightless wooden airplane grow unreasonably large, straining at the confines of his apartment like a huge bird hatching from an egg. One wing was pushing into the dining nook, the other was angled so that it flapped out of an open window like a waving hand. The fuselage had gotten so long that he had to prop open the balcony door, pushing the nose of the plane outside; awkward and strange, but in his view a more humane creation than shopping malls and cars strung tight as beads along the QEW, one that would calm the memory of strafings and dogfights and crashing planes, all those things that for years had stood between him and a wild, excruciating howl of loneliness. Only he wasn't in the cockpit any more, he was alone in his room as he'd always been, not sure how to get on with his life or what to do with his creation and the memories it kept drawing out of him.

He wanted Christina to see the plane; he figured she could already sense what its creation meant to him. When she stepped into his apartment, she walked right up to the model and let her hand rest gently on a wing, as if she were greeting an old acquaintance.

"The plane's so beautiful, it wants you to fly it," she said. Terry looked away.

"The wings weren't meant to fly," he answered.

"You can't be sure," Christina said. Terry remembered her paintings that brought his room to life; they weren't meant to do that, either.

"I'll never fly again," Terry answered. "I'll never leave this room again."

"Don't sulk," Christina said. "The breeze dies down when you're glum."

Terry smiled a little, then glanced at her paintings on the wall. He realized everything in the room was stirring with the same invisible life: the airplane, Christina's artwork; she was nudging the whole room awake. He looked at her, his eyes scared.

"I don't like it when everything starts breathing like that," Terry said. He felt embarrassed and uneasy having to admit it.

"Then why did you make something so alive?" Christina asked.

Terry barely heard her. Memories were starting to move through him as if he were a membrane that could breathe them in and out, and he felt afraid when he saw the walls opening to the blue sky, himself in the cockpit on the day of the accident, where just before the engine fired, he reached over and grabbed Helen's hand, felt instead an instrument, a routine part of the pre-flight check and not a hand, so that his own felt lifeless and empty.

"Why are you looking at your hands, Terry?" Christina asked.

Without knowing why, he'd opened them, spread them wide, saw his fingers long and pale, the skin very white, the fine blue veins like branches of trees and rivers, themselves veins in the vast, invisible body of the world, only he didn't rest easily in the web of these connections.

"I'm remembering flying," he said. "What your hands are supposed to tell you."

He reached over and took some of the strands of her long red hair between his fingers, examining them as if they were not hair at all, but something rare and unfamiliar he hadn't seen before: copper filaments, precious metal milled to a thinness and softness he could not have imagined.

"It's real hair," Christina said.

Hesitant at first, he lifted the strands, then very slowly raised them to his lips and kissed them.

*

Terry sat with his hands covering his face, the feel of
Christina's hair still soft on his fingers; he had no idea how
long he'd been sitting like this. He heard her voice; it had
a bright and tiny ring to it, like fine crystal lightly touched.

"Are you asleep, Terry?" she asked him. He shook
his head, still drifting through the shadows before his eyes
until he moved into the place where he'd crashed his plane,
into the sound of a big twig snapping under the weight of
heavy feet, as if he were still listening, barely conscious, for
his rescuers. Terry felt his lips move as they had then, felt
words begin to take form, only this time the syllables broke
into small crumbling bits like pebbles sliding down a cliff.
It was his father's name; the name was dust. He heard the
last of it, eddies of sound dissolving into air, moving
through walls that parted, opening wide so that he could
see the blueness of the sky and feel the strange, gentle quiet
of the world as he had never known it. He felt sure it was
the breeze; Christina, weightless and floating through his
mind as if he too were a window open to the sky, as if she
herself were lighting on his thoughts, small and graceful,
almost flying.

"It's the plane that's moving the air like that," she
said. Christina stood up and turned towards the painted
fuselage, gold strands of late-noon sun glinting in her
coppery hair. Then she reached over and took his hand.
He looked at her, then felt afraid, unprotected, teetering
on the edge of the sky: in flight without a plane or wings.
Christina was tugging at the wood-and-paper doorframe
to the cockpit.

"Just for fun, come on," she said, pulling him

towards the door. He felt embarrassed. He'd built the cockpit as a replica, an exercise in precision modelling; he'd never meant to be childish, to play at flying. He shrugged, , then climbed in after her, pulling the door shut behind him. Instinctively, Terry felt careful with this plane, more wary; none of the old, tight, energetic movements, the metallic slamming of the cockpit door; none of the relentless noisy throb of flying. Everything inside this space was absolutely quiet, so still he felt sure that if he stopped to listen, he'd hear the plane breathing. He closed his eyes, opened them again, saw blue sky through the cockpit, wondered if he was dreaming, imagining the gentle lift in the seat, the plane shedding memory from its wings as it moved like air through open windows, through walls that were thin membranes breathing it in and out.

"Chris, what's going on?" he whispered. Christina took his hand and held it between hers; then she put her arm around his shoulder, reminding him that he had made this plane. It was of his body, the lightness was of him.

*

Only now the plane was no longer alive.

Terry touched the fuselage, feeling in the beauty of his creation a huge, dead carapace slipping from his body; its brittleness dry and papery, frail as an insect's wings. The plane, he knew, would eventually fall apart, shrivel up like old thoughts he'd grown tired of thinking. He felt unexpected grief as he told Christina this. She looked at him kindly.

"Sit still, Terry," she said. "Think of the breeze." Terry held her hand, drifting inside her stillness, floating like a river through the strange and gentle quiet.

MOONWALKERS

This is how Helen knows she is above the ground; she sees the tall grass swaying, knows there must be rhythms to go with the movement of the air. She thinks of the sound of water lapping against the tidal flats, only the rotor blades above her head are chopping the blue sky into hard, noisy little bits, and the dancing grass on the other side of the plastic bubble pulls away, bowing low before the sweep of the helicopter as it clears the ground and lifts her into the sky. She doesn't mind the noise; she hardly notices when the grass disappears.

Helen is not afraid to fly over the wilderness of the Queen Charlotte Islands even though she feels she should be. She waits for her nerve endings to topple her through the plexiglas bubble of the cockpit but nothing happens. Wanting to be transparent, thin as air, she is moving above the hangars at Sandspit into the bush; she lets the racket of the engine swallow her body whole, feeling safe without bones or flesh. The chopper is bobbing gently up and down above the green points of cedar and hemlock; feeling this, Helen remembers when she was a girl on holidays in

South Moresby, how her mother researched botanical specimens and her father made notes on birds and trees and native artifacts because he was a judge and this was his habit, making notes. Helen grew up in British Columbia, knows the islands well, but isn't sure why she's come back here. She is an engineer, more interested in flight than in rare vegetation and ancient ruins.

Helen doesn't know the helicopter pilot well because she only met him yesterday. The man is lanky, well built, sandy hair sticking out from the trim edges of a helmet, a long and bony face; the blue eyes attentive to his flying are aloof, occasionally puzzled. He wears a silver-grey windbreaker with a NASA patch on the sleeve showing an American flag and an astronaut walking on the moon. Helen has asked him to take her to Anthony Island. Last night he bought her a drink in the bar at Sandspit, and afterwards she began moving through his body, her eyes taking off his clothing and his skin so that the man sitting next to her is now transparent, a moving image like a hologram. She can put her hand right through him into the cold bright air of northern Ontario, into the cockpit of Terry's Cessna, where she can touch the worn skin of her old friend's leather jacket, see his blond hair and grey eyes bleached by light so that they look harmed by it, like overexposed film. She can feel how Terry held her in his arms on the tarmac at North Bay Airport, buried his face in her hair as if he were sinking into its warmth and wouldn't come out. Her dark hair is short now; the curves of her body have a new geometry of flat surfaces and angles. Having left Terry, she feels him part of her, too close, as if it were his skin that covered the fine bones of her face. She is becoming a lantern and her eyes a deep blue core of light; anyone can look inside her, see nightmares like shadows moving through her bones.

Below her is wilderness, not so different from the bush around North Bay where Terry lost his plane, let it fall on them both like a knife; him in the cockpit laughing and whistling silvery arcs of sound that ended in little explosions, tiny bombs meant for his father, who abandoned him when he was still a kid; swooping and diving as if his old man were the sky. She should have told him imagination was the safest place to fight a war and he should quit taking chances, but she didn't. She liked his craziness that had its own passion: the gritty feel of striking a match, the moment of absolute stillness before it catches fire.

*

As the chopper banks, Helen sees Anthony Island; her eyes pluck it loose from the ocean and tilt it sideways as if it were a large blue-green cube she could hold in her hands. The pilot says they are approaching the ruin of Ninstints village. Helen knows the history of this place, how a century ago Europeans brought smallpox here and all the Indians died or fled, leaving behind only what the plane tilts back and forth at a distance: the sweep of ink-blue water narrowing into the rocky channel and the stretch of cove and sandy beach, the wooden poles the Haida built to honour their dead. They are adorned with weathered carvings of giant mythic birds inside the moon, whales with frogs under their fins, beavers with human faces on their tails; moving figures born and reborn inside each others' bodies with the certainty of life that does not believe in death, their massive eyes cracked and split open with too much seeing of wind and sea air. Helen thinks these sturdy creatures will see and judge her frailty; she suddenly feels she shouldn't land. She thinks she'll never land anywhere. Maybe she's dead and this is her hell, not landing.

She counts three grey rubber dinghies below, seven or eight tiny people with backpacks and camping gear sitting on white logs that slice the beach like scars on a face. Helen eyes them, hears a crackle in her headset. The pilot's voice as he makes another pass over the island is terse, faintly amused.

"Naturalists, they don't like us coming here," he says. "We lack a certain something."

"Just keep circling then," Helen says. "Don't land."

"And run out of fuel?" he answers. "No law says we can't land."

Helen feels in her pocket; she has two passes from the band office in Skidegate. They remind her of yesterday when she got permission for them to fly here; this is her only tangible evidence, other than the pilot, that yesterday even was. They are banking low enough now to see faces looking upward, their eyes full of hostility and fear. Helen has seen all this before, knows these are people who imagine themselves gentle, not like pilots of noisy choppers with their resonance of bullets and napalm. Terry used to look pained flying over scenes like this; she sees the same discomfort in the pilot's eyes.

The helicopter lands on a stretch of sandy beach at the north end of the village. Helen and the pilot both wait before opening the doors; the rotor blade above them is still revolving, slicing chunks of air. As she looks up ahead,

Helen sees the group of naturalists walking towards them. They move lightly, as if they were riding on air above the beach. They are drifting around the chopper like ground-level fog, only it's smoke she sees, not fog: the crackle of a fire that never goes out, the force of impact throwing her forward out of the plane; her bones cracking and splintering like shards of glass against hard rock, and the warm taste of blood in her mouth before she blacks out, comes to, sees the calm eyes of men and women inspecting the scene from a distance. Some wearing army fatigues and carrying stretchers edge closer, while others step back into the shadows where her father makes notes and judges and her mother examines rare botanical specimens of the Pre-Cambrian Shield. Helen cries out to them; feels silence through the blind, white grip of pain.

*

She sits in the cockpit with her face in her hands, sure she'll be sick unless she gets some fresh air, but she can't see the man whose arm is leaning against the door. She finally looks up, reaches for the handle, and pushes the door open as far as she can; then she notices a pale-looking man with a beard and moustache and frizzy hair dark as coal-dust, so that if she touched it, she feels sure it would crumble and leave soot on her fingers. Helen is not entirely convinced that he's real. She traces his face on the plexiglas with her finger, lets her eyes soften the edges of his body as if she were drawing him in charcoal, watches as he blurs into her memory of a man named Stephen whom she left five years earlier for Terry. Stephen, so dense with thought and worry that a teaspoonful of him would weigh as much as the earth he meant to save; Helen moves through this man in front of her, collides with Stephen's body like a miner's pick striking rock.

"You got permission to be here?" the man asks.

Helen removes her passes from her breast pocket, then holds them up for the man to see, feeling his eyes on her body as she does this. She is supposed to give them to the Haida watchman from the band office. She asks this man if he knows where to find him. He shakes his head no, then gestures absently towards the bush.

"Somewhere in there," he says.

She knows enough not to turn over the passes; she slips them back in her pocket. Yes, she has permission, she explains; even so she is starting to feel she has no business being here. She still lives frozen inside the memory of flying with Terry, ripping a hole in the sky and setting the bush on fire. No longer innocent, she feels she carries some nameless harm with her, except that she's been to Ninstints before, knows about the fragile vegetation and not to step on burial sites, and all at once she's angry at this man whose voice is an echo of her own. Who the hell do you think you are, she wonders. I don't owe you an explanation.

Yes you do, his eyes say. They are expressionless, dark like stones under water.

"You like flying?" he asks.

She nods, yes, most of the time she does.

"I don't," he answers. "Speaks to an ethic of distance from nature."

Now Helen smiles. The guy's so much like Stephen; even in bed he used to talk politics, load her up with random passion for one cause or another as if he were pumping his car full of premium gas. Besides, Stephen never cared much for engineering and flying. Helen, he used to say, I love you so much I wouldn't want to see you get hurt, and then he'd tell her she needed to be protected from accidents and the technological arrogance of her profession and besides that, he couldn't bear to lose her. Helen remembers it was the first time she ever meant that much to a man, but eventually she yanked herself out from under Stephen's flattery and left him. Now it seemed he'd sent along a guy just like himself to chase her down, Stephen with the pretence of concern scraped off, only the hard rock bare in him, of wanting things his way.

Helen decides to ignore the charcoal-haired man. She glances at the pilot, who looks bemused, a big grin tugging at the corners of his eyes. He holds up two fingers in a V.

"'We come in peace for all mankind,'" he quotes, flashing his NASA badge.

"You came to the wrong place, this isn't the fucking moon, pal," the man says. The pilot looks annoyed and Helen is starting to feel nervous.

"We'll wait for the watchman," she answers.

"In the meantime, I could entertain you by listing the toxic pollutants in aircraft fuel," the man says, opening the door an inch wider. Helen sits up straight like a student in class.

"Benzene, toluene, aromatic hydrocarbons," she recites. "Carcinogenic. Damage to the central nervous system. Do I get an A?"

"Lighten up, you guys," the pilot says. The man scowls and says nothing. Helen smiles, remembering the most unlucky day of Stephen's life, how he took her out with him to picket a factory in Toronto where they made precision instruments for aircraft that choked up the sky with carbon emissions and burst the eardrums of native hunters; that was how she met Terry, who worked there and whose car broke down at the plant gate. Helen told Terry she was an engineer, helped him fix his car, learned he was a pilot, hopped in, drove off, and left Stephen for ever. Thinking about this, Helen feels cooped up all over again, in need of fresh air. She grips the door handle and pushes out, but the man who looks like Stephen has his weight against it, pushing in the opposite direction.

"Would you please move," she says.

"You need permission from the watchman," he answers.

"We'll wait for him outside," she says. The man smiles.

"I'm in charge here, permission denied." He slams the door, slouching against it so she can't get out.

Helen knows he's not in charge, and she can always crawl out the pilot's side, but she can't move; she's scared of falling head first into the man's eyes. They are expressionless, obsidian, she's going to slam into the hard rock; she stares at the pilot, wonders why he doesn't make a move. Only now he's Terry, the sun in his blond hair catching fire as he swoops over the bush, dancing on the edge of sanity, and she's yelling go for it and laughing, until some huge prehistoric bat-winged Canadian Forces fighter comes roaring up at them, chopping the sky in half; Terry keeps making his bank too steep, keeps spiralling downward through the long darkness of her body. His plane is forever about to crash, poised like a dancer in its midair spin before it breaks apart in the stone-black eyes of this man before her. On Anthony Island, time is stranded in the present, beached like a dead whale; Stephen is watching her suffer, he is forever having his revenge on her life.

Helen hears the thud of her own fists banging on the door of the plane, her voice yelling that he'd better let them out or she'll report them all to the band office. The dark-haired man on the other side of the plexiglas looks startled, then steps aside and lets her open the cockpit door. Relieved, Helen swings her legs down and drops to the ground. Just as she lands, she feels his hand in her breast pocket, he's got the passes; before she can stop him, he rips them up and tosses the scraps of paper into the waters of the bay. Helen is too stunned to say anything. The pilot takes a deep breath, clenching and unclenching his fists.

"I'm going to find the watchman," he says. "I'm having you kicked off the island, buddy." The man shrugs.

"I respect the ground," he answers. "This place doesn't need any more fucking over." He stares hard at Helen, then walks away.

She feels sick, sure they told her in Skidegate it was okay for the chopper to land here, only she isn't landing; she doesn't know what it means to respect the ground when it won't even hold her up. She keeps falling right through the earth, down into clouds and blue sky, and she's terrified she'll never be allowed to land; after that she remembers nothing until she opens her eyes. She's lying on the beach next to the helicopter, staring up at the sky that dropped her here; the pilot is crouching by her side and the man who tore up the passes is pacing back and forth as if he were a sentinel guarding a prisoner. A woman camper is observing her; she looks serene, her skin pale white and her eyes as cool as cut-glass chips of blue sky.

Helen can smell the fresh scent of pine on her skin, cedar and woodland flowers; she's been collecting rare specimens. As she opens her eyes, Helen feels this woman in the hollow of her suffering, wants her to understand everything that's happened, only she sees her eyes narrow; they have ice-blue cracks in them, they are examining the broken part of her as if this woman were a surgeon about to set a bone. Helen feels a tingle of cold like the hard slap of an ocean wave, involuntarily covers her eyes, then feels a hand on her arm. It's the pilot; he's asking everyone to move aside. He's looking at her, concern in his eyes.

The pilot helps her to her feet, tells her some fresh air will make her feel better; she's been cooped up to long. Helen lets him take her by the arm. He tells her he wants to find the Haida watchman who was supposed to take their passes; she wonders if the man has vanished into the folds and ripples of this island as if it were a mind that had forgotten him. Maybe she'll vanish, too; maybe she's not real and the dead are thinking her, thin and transparent as fog drifting before the great carved eyes of totems. She walks slowly, one step at a time, across the curve of the white beach and the green rise of forest and ancient ruins; she's holding the pilot's hand because their feet touch lightly on the ground, sometimes don't touch at all. Weightless, she reaches through his skin, the silver-grey of his astronaut's jacket; feels Terry lying in bed where she left him because they were mortal and she was afraid of death. Floating inside him she feels herself step and rise, step and rise across the rocks and water of this unknown country, move inside the weathered totems, the fins and claws of beasts with human eyes; through the trunks of trees and the forms of wandering spirits until she is a bird with the face of the moon, bodiless, all eyes, frail as light. She is inside the mystery of flying; she does not walk easily upon this earth.

THIS IS FOR MANDY

Our daughter Mandy is twenty-five years old, desperate to know how she came to be born in Canada, in darkness, in the nerve-dead cold of winter. What she wants are words that hum like engines, driving a story she already knows, pulling it across vast distances: my face, Jeremy's eyes, old grief as unassailable as mountains.

When Mandy was sixteen, I caught her sniffing the pages of a textbook, American history. I asked her why, and she said for the jasmine, and I laughed, but Mandy didn't. My wedding flower, jasmine, plucked from a bush that her namesake planted, her grandmother who died when Jeremy was born. This is the history that Mandy is searching for: what the body knows in its breathing, in its hands that touch unbroken threads, the needlework of stories. Only Jeremy and I have had to stitch and mend our lives, the ragged cloth that history has made of them, one that protects us from all that the body remembers.

Mandy knows that we came to Canada, which is not the same as what our bodies know: that we were blown here, two leaves in a gale-force wind. I'm pregnant, I told

Jeremy, nineteen and feeling the electric hiss of fright in him, but his fear was of death, not of birth. He had just gotten his draft notice, feeling in it the end of his life, punishment for the loss of his mother's. His hand drifting across my cheek, I love you, Sarah, you're not scared? I told him I wanted the child, that I would make in myself a space for it larger than death.

We married and left for Canada, left my family, crisp as flags, stiff and unforgiving; left Jeremy's father alone. He had another son in Vietnam, yet he never spoke his pain or worry. Quiet he was, like a footprint in the snow. When we left, he watched us from the window, saying nothing.

Scared crossing the border, signing forms for the pale Canadian guard who questioned us in a road-flat voice, who handed us our papers and said, you'll need warmer coats'n what you got on, eh, and he told us about Eaton's. Back in the car, Jeremy's eyes filled with the image of his father's face through windows, the silent grief of it. The kindness of a stranger made him weep.

I took his hand and put it on my stomach. Feel, Jer, I said, and he kept his hand where the child was, the future that he didn't know, the thread that was for mending, breaking: death and birth.

And this is for Mandy because she is alive, because Jeremy's brother didn't return from the war and his father is gone, because we were a rain that the soil of Canada drank, the past ebbing away from us like water to the sea.

THE MEMORY WALL

Rudy is straddling the balcony railing, riding it like a motorbike, a beer bottle in his free hand, suds gushing down his arm. He looks like he's holding a hand grenade with the pin out.

"I'll wash. You dry!" he yells at the neighbours' satellite dish. He's swaying. From his perch, Rudy looks like he's headed straight for the centre of the cone. I come running, grab his arm, and pull him back.

"You want to kill yourself?" I ask him.

"Not right this minute, thanks," he mumbles, as if he might take me up on it later. Looking chagrined, he lets me help him off the railing. This is all I need: Rudy bonkers, pissed out of his skull, the only guy in Meredith Point who wants to wash a satellite dish. Maybe he sees a laundry tub the size of a parking lot. It's filled with dirty satellite dishes, the grime of wars and soccer riots and stock-market crashes soaking out into the tepid grey water. I still have his arm as I get him into his room.

"What the hell did you do that for?" I say. Rudy sits slumped over in a chair, his face in his hands. He looks about forty, but his hair has gone the grey of cigarette ash. Very slowly he sits up, as if he were toting a sack of bricks on his shoulders.

"Two hundred channels," he says. "Maximum concentrated blowout. A bunch of little wires in the brain, all fried." There is pain in his stare, his eyes spilling a great slick of darkness into the room.

"Rudy, I don't follow," I say. He smiles a little. "I'm sorry," he says. "I keep forgetting you're a TV star."

"Well, not exactly."

I'm in from Toronto, here to line up a few interviews for a long-weekend TV news filler. Here's the story: Americans in a New York City suburb take stock this Independence Day, in a post–Desert Storm, dead-of-winter economy. Rudy's on my pre-interview list; he isn't sure he can handle the real thing on camera. He says he might feel better about it if I did the interview. It might work out; it might not. He'd be a convenient and interesting choice; he's a tenant in Ma's old house, a Vietnam vet.

Rudy knew my cousin, who didn't come back from the war. That's how he ended up here; adrift, he managed to keep in touch with my aunt, who wove him into the kindness of her family, into a caretaker's job with Ma and a rented room he made his home. But now he's got me worried; he's supposed to be keeping an eye on the place, not cracking up on the concrete down below.

The late sunlight melts into the corner of a scratched bureau, softens the tip of a small American flag. Outside, there is light on the wooden railing of the balcony where Rudy almost fell, the paint on it peeling away like sunburnt skin. There are framed pictures on the bookcase,

Ma's old photos: yellowing pictures of me with my cousins, my grandparents, and aunts; First Communions, graduations, weddings, all of it delicate, brittle with memory; protected under glass, as if it would disintegrate in fresh air and sunlight. The photos sit alongside Rudy's medals from Vietnam. At home with Ma, he's placed them here as if he were a cousin, one whose story, painful as it is, has a rightful place in our lives. Along with the medals, he's put news clippings on the walls: lots of feature articles and coloured graphics. Everywhere there was space to fill, he's put columns, photo spreads on every subject, night-black headlines from the invasion of Kuwait, the Gulf War. The room feels close with memory and suffering, as if someone had built a nest, patched it together with scraps of trouble.

"Talk about frying your brains, what is this mess?" I ask him. He looks puzzled.

"It's my memory wall," he says. "Helps me remember what's going on, otherwise I lose it."

"You could save more stuff with a VCR," I tell him.

"'Outta sight, outta mind,' want it in front of me, right here," he says. "I read someplace how TV kills the memory-bits in the brain."

"Don't believe it," I say. "At the end of a rough day, you remember plenty."

And you're trying to line this guy up for an interview, I tell myself. A sixties-vintage vet finds an interesting, offbeat way of dealing with the New Reality, the New World, whatever the fancy slogan is for too much information. As I'm thinking this, Rudy gets up, hunts through a box of newspaper clippings on his bureau, finds what he wants, and hands it to me—a page ripped out of the New York *Daily News*. MAN AXES TUBE IN

—84—

PROTEST, the headline reads. The picture shows Rudy by the curbside in front of a house, wielding his blade, slicing through the trim plastic body of his set, splinters of glass caught and held in the photo like dancing bits of ice in a blizzard, and him saying he'd had enough mindless garbage, sex and violence, and like the guy in the old *Network* movie he was as mad as hell. I shake my head, puzzled. Rudy, what are you up to? I can feel the thought like a printout moving from my eyes across my face, easy enough for him to read. His voice is quiet; aimless, like snow drifting.

"Too much Gulf War; I lost it," he says. He glances at his hands, palms outward, as if he could read some explanation for his suffering in their strange crisscross of thick and bumpy scars. I reach out and touch them; they seem in need of touching.

"You hurt yourself, smashing up the TV?" I ask him.

"Vietnam," he says.

"I'm sorry," I tell him.

"TV made me think of it, that's all," he answers.

*

Last fall, Ma died; her old house is now mine, a convenience while I'm down here on assignment. Rudy putters away around the place, tends to the lawn and garden, earns his living doing patios and decks and paving-stone driveways for invisible neighbours, the cell-phone and fax crowd, absentee parents whose kids grow up listening to CDs, to voices in their headsets, no other sounds. It's true that Meredith Point has always been a quiet place, protected behind tall fences, far from trouble, as if it were afraid of its country's sufferings, of the weight of the history it carries inside it like an ominous shadow on an X-ray. Thin black borders around the edges of our lives, wounds that do not heal are invisible here.

I think of Rudy, of the war he carries in the thick, tight skin of his hands. Then I remember Greg, who fled with me to Canada, a place austere and splendid enough for him, a man with ideals as unassailable as the sides of cliffs. Years ago, I would have frowned on Rudy and the way he let himself get drafted, dumped into a war like a load of garbage into a landfill. Now I'm not so arrogant. I like to think that since my marriage ended, I've become more sympathetic towards all that is rough and ill formed; human like myself. I wonder what it is Rudy wants from memory, awash as he is in the same river that spills its banks every time I write news copy about some one-size-fits-all civil war in Central Asia, Central Africa, Central America. Rudy the eye of a hurricane, civilizing the weeds out of lawns, making the fresh paint gleam on a window ledge, setting down bone-white pots of geraniums red as blood; sitting before his memory wall, his back bent under the years of silence.

*

Rudy's display takes up the west side of his room, covering two walls and the dormers that arch around his balcony door. There are hundreds of clippings, new events tacked on top of old to form layers of newsprint and magazine copy, thick, clotted wads of paper, Post-it notes to the conscience. It's a clutter, a curious puzzle. He smiles at me.

"You never wondered where old stories go when they're too old for TV?" he asks.

"Always thought they ended up in outer space," I tell him.

In fact, I've never thought about stories as if they had destinations, inner lives, growing in the medium of television as plants do in soil, then drying out into husks, seeds, tiny spores borne on the air, returning to life on Rudy's wall. Maybe this is why I see before me a shrivelled carapace, a shell; all that remains of dictators, serial killers, innocent victims of wars and famines and natural disasters, people I've thought have wriggled out of their stories and fled long ago. Maybe there's more to Rudy's obsession, something invisible to me. I decide to investigate which subjects he's clipped most often, just to see if there's some pattern, some cohesion to what feels too much like madness.

I reach out to touch a grainy photo, a naked screaming little Vietnamese kid, a human grenade doused with gasoline and set alight. I remember this child: years ago Greg taped the picture to the wall, and it frightened me because I couldn't contain her with metaphor: a charred piece of toast, the ember of a cigarette, no, none of these. Sheets of loose burning skin slipping from her body like ill-fitting clothes, all of us naked in the shame of watching her suffer.

Rudy's staring at me. "You just did a fade, what's wrong?" he asks. I tell him nothing's wrong. He crouches down beside me.

"Something on the wall? What?"

"It's the wall, period, Rudy. You've got to take it down." Rudy stares at me, as if he hopes I'll disappear.

"Waddya mean, take it down?"

"It's dangerous, Rudy, a fire hazard. Some of this stuff is getting mouldy."

"Ain't a five-star restaurant," he says.

"It's my home," I answer.

"You mean after the interview, take it down. You want your story first, right?"

"That's not fair."

"What ain't fair? Fuckin' misery marchin' 'cross your face like an army, and you give me some shit about my walls? What the hell, Angie, loosen up, you're home."

I didn't expect this from him. It's years since I've thought of this place as home. Maybe I should just admit I'm shaken. I try, then I point to the picture that upset me. His gaze darkens as he bends down to look at it. Slowly he reaches out to touch the image of the burning child, his injured hands as sensitive as a blind man's to texture and contour, as if he were desperate to know the name and meaning of what his fingers are holding.

"It's so horrible," I say to him. His hand is still resting on the picture of the child.

"Who woulda hurt a kid that way?" he says.

"Why're you keeping it, Rudy?"

"Somebody gotta feel shame," he answers. "If it'd been me done that, I'd of killed myself."

"I'd throw it out," I tell him.

"You don't get rid of things, throwin' 'em out." Then he puts a hand on my arm and whispers so that I can barely hear him. "You think I'm crazy, please don't treat me like a fuck-up, Angie. Something bugging you, talk to me, huh; I'm human."

It's the end of the distance between us, twenty years

of exile breaking inside me as I speak.

*

(Only the child on fire never stops burning, that's what the picture shows you; Greg in his compassion and rage said that often enough. Get an eyeful of this picture and this picture, but I was a sheltered kid, eighteen years old; I wasn't ready to witness atrocities, to know the horrific things that humans are capable of doing. One day I broke down, took a batch of Greg's antiwar posters, tore them to pieces, shredded them, returning them to him, to the white, frosted breath of his silence, telling him I couldn't bear to live with these.

That night I went wandering in a snowstorm, lost and numbed with cold. When I finally made my way back home, I told him everything I felt, told him I was sorry about the pictures, got him scared enough to wrap me up in a blanket, give me whisky and comfort. Only our marriage finally came apart, the slim bones of it breaking under the weight of loss and exile. For a while I tried to sleep inside his nightmares, inside the burning of Southeast Asian jungles, but I'd had enough of wandering through so much pain. I wanted to dissolve his pictures into motes of dust on a beam of light, into television, oblivion, a good forgetting.)

*

"Greg and I thought we were heroes, running away," I tell Rudy later. He lights a cigarette and takes a drag.

"Us too," he says. "Me 'n' your cousin. Bunch of

fuckin' heroes." Both of us fall silent. Rudy puts his cigarette down and leans back on his bed. "You still want me to talk?" he asks.

"How do you mean, Rudy?"

"Your interview. You think I got something to say?"

I look at him and answer yes, of course, touched and surprised by the question, as if he's asking me to tell him what he's worth. "You're not put off by the camera?" I ask him. Rudy looks away, smiling a little. "No more'n you're put off by the wall," he says.

He asks if I'll interview him, and I say I'm sure they'll let me. They won't know I've lost the appropriate distance from my subject. I tell him it would be a fine interview if he could talk about Vietnam, how it relates to his wall, to his feelings about television. He looks pensive, doesn't speak, takes a long drag, butts out his cigarette.

"To my shrink I talk about that," he says. I pause, surprised.

"Have you been ill, Rudy?" I ask him.

"Nah, just crazy. Like I said, don't remember hardly nuthin' from those days. Don't look so shocked, Jesus."

"I'm not shocked," I tell him. Rudy puts an awkward hand on mine.

"I should keep my fucking trap shut," he says. "My own damn fault my brains were fried. We were kids then, what did we know, huh?" His words hold the weight of something terrible, a memory of gunfire, the crack of it still breaking in his voice.

We knew nothing, Rudy; nothing.

I feel his lips resting on my hair, then on my

forehead. He stops, asks if it's okay. I nod, tell him with my eyes that we are both in need of comfort. Rudy's lips barely rest on my mouth, like skin that is raw and hurts to the touch. It surprises me how slowly he undresses, as if he were shy and had never loved a woman before; then I see that his arms and chest are thick with the ropes and knots of scars, burn marks. How constrained he looks because of it, his flesh tugged and pulled tight in odd places as if he were bound in a strait-jacket, a prisoner of his own skin. I find myself weeping.

"I asked for it, please don't feel sorry for me," he whispers.

I don't know why I'm crying. I tell him this as I take his hand, press the palm of it to my lips, letting my tongue move over the thick scars until I am beyond the skin, inside; moving within charred walls blackened with memory; I touch his bones until I smell smoke and taste it on my tongue. Rudy, where are we, I wonder, afraid of the world's horror settled in our bodies like the toxic silt of a thousand poisoned rivers; afraid the world is dreaming us, setting fire to our bones.

*

Rudy's room is thick with cable, all of it taped to the floor, anchoring the metal braces of cameras and lights. The two of us make our way past the semicircle of lighting and camera techs setting up gear in front of the wall of newsprint. We sit down, facing them. We are dusted with makeup; tested for lighting, asked to speak into our mikes, told to notice when the red light of the camera blinks on.

I find serenity in this ritual, peace in knowing what

they expect of me. Rudy, of course, does not. He looks anxious, frozen. I want to take his hand, but I can't. It's okay, I say with my eyes. This will be unnerving, the shift from intimacy to detachment, this complication invisible to the camera; I'm not sure what it will mean for my questions once they leave the page, once they move as close to Rudy as his own breath. The producer gives me a hand signal; there's the red light. I begin by introducing Rudy, describing his wall as the camera pans across it, asking him to explain what got him started hoarding scraps of news.

"Got sick and tired of forgetting it all," Rudy says, looking right into the camera. "This is my space, the lining of my brain, right?"

"Is there some reason why you kept forgetting?" I ask him.

"Too damn much news," Rudy answers.

"There had to be one thing in particular that made you axe your tube," I say to him. He smiles. "I lost it watching Desert Storm," he says.

"Lost what? Can you say more?" All these one-liners; it feels foolish pressing him, but I move ahead with my questions, flushing out answers with the instinctive reflex of a TV pro, as if I were nothing more than an eye blinking, cleansing itself of grime. These are things the audience will want to know, I tell myself. Only Rudy is silent, his eyes lowered. Finally he speaks.

"Lost it," he says, his voice soft. "Just plain fucking lost it." Not anger in his voice, but the nuance of grief, regret, the kind of private comment that ignores the presence of a camera. Yet I can't ignore it; I have to listen, to hear more than he's saying, to ask what I don't understand.

"It must be difficult for you to talk about this," I say. The camera moves in on Rudy, who nods, lowers his eyes, says nothing.

"Maybe you could show us around the wall, instead." Rudy gets up very slowly, the harsh light turning his face blank, impassive as a suspect posing for his mug shot. I put my hand on the clippings, wonder if I am imagining the odd sensation of decay, rotting fibre, leaves. He begins to loosen up, to talk about the stories on his wall: Lockerbie, Exxon Valdez, Bhopal, the Gulf War. I listen, ask questions, touch these clippings, feel myself moving dreamlike into the texture of physical loss, into a power capable of holding me inside the scorched upholstery of airplane seats, inside choking gulls, oil slicks, an omnipresent fire. Questions, moist fronds of paper, jungle. We go further back into Rudy's wall. Years part like underbrush, dark paths tunnel into his mind. The camera lights recede, blur and shimmer as if I were seeing them through windows streaked with rain.

I am asking Rudy questions, my fingers reaching, touching the place on the wall where the story begins; Rudy saying Angela, I just plain fucking lost it. Old grainy photos come alive at my touch, loose flesh hangs ragged from the bodies of the dead like moss from trees. Bodies lurch, fall into mass graves, their skin drenched with gasoline and lit by a man on a bulldozer ploughing them into the mud. He's faceless, no one in particular, an understudy in the drama, doing whatever it is Rudy remembers with his injured hands. An old word comes to my mind from the Middle Ages, a palimpsest, one text written on top of another, buried truth hiding. I can ask questions, put my hand through this anonymous photo, touch the flesh and bone of what really happened to the man before me. I don't blame Rudy that he's afraid of this.

Angela, I just plain fucking lost it.

His scarred hands know whatever it is his mind won't accept, floating in slow motion through the space he calls the lining of his brain, his back to the cameras as he throws his arms against the wall, raking his fingers through the scraps of brittle paper. Shredded clippings bunch in his hands, tangle around his fingers. He throws them on the floor, turns around, faces the camera, and opens his hands wide like a magician who's made an object disappear. I come to attention, ask again what the audience needs to know.

"Rudy, what are you doing to the wall?"

"What does it look like?" he answers.

"But you're tearing it up, why?" I ask. He pauses, talks right into the camera.

"You took the brain right outta my head," he says to it. "You seen too much."

He turns his back again, rips off another clump of newsprint, then another. The camera is relentless, following him with its eye as he trudges out of the room. Great stuff, the producer tells me later. Great television. Unbelievable, that guy.

*

Rudy sits on the edge of the bed, his head bowed, hands clasped tightly together, as if his thoughts were clay he could mould into shape with his fingers. As he opens his hands, wads of paper fall from them and drop to the floor, bunched-up news clippings.

"Sorry I fucked up," he says. He doesn't look at me.

"I shouldn't have put you through that," I tell him.
"Truth don't hurt to know."

The truth, according to Rudy, is that he'll never retrieve what he forgot and lost in Vietnam long ago. In any case, memory is something for computer disks and tapes to tally up, for satellite dishes to grind to smithereens as they touch down like twisters in the fields of the New World. That kind of memory hurts less than the real thing, anyway. Maybe he'll even buy himself another television.

He asks me if I'll help him peel away the rest of his wall, the loose shreds of tribal warfare, job layoffs, toxic spills. I nod yes but say nothing, feeling uneasy, just as I did the night he nearly fell from the balcony. All of this brittle paper is Rudy, all that I know of his mind, his painstaking reconstruction of memory, the pieces of it spliced with the care of a surgeon grafting skin to burns, a history he gave himself so he wouldn't go mad when he saw the scars and remembered nothing. I thought this as he picks up a clipping showing the oil fires of Kuwait, his eyes lighting with recognition and fear.

"What is it, Rudy?"

I rub his shoulders, his back, the scars that have become his body, his skin, the lost part of his mind that cannot begin to name the horror that it sees.

*

When all the clippings are down, Rudy stuffs two garbage bags full of shredded newspaper and pulls them onto the balcony. Puzzled by this, I ask him what he's doing. What he's doing is staring down at the genteel town of Meredith Point, the respectable place he has mowed and clipped and seeded, dreaming itself under the shade trees into a coastal summer day of lazy noon and humming cicadas. He is staring across the neighbour's yard at the satellite dish.

"Place needs sprucing up," he says.

He yanks open the first bag, grabs handfuls of brittle paper, and starts sprinkling them over the lawns. I grab his arm and yank him back.

"Rudy, you're crazy."

"You noticed." He takes the garbage bag and dumps the whole thing over the balcony railing.

The paper rides on the warm air as it begins to disintegrate in the bright sunlight, crumbling and flaking until the sky is thick with fragments. Not only the sky but the ground below, as if the sloughed-off skin of the earth were rising up under the lawns, up from the flowerbeds, from whole countries built on landfills of prodigal, undigested memory, its poisons leaching into the streams and watercourses of the earth; up from the countless hurts and sufferings for which no one has felt shame or asked forgiveness. And then I wonder if I'm dreaming this, if I'm still in bed with Rudy, pressing my lips to his hand, my tongue moving through his scars, tasting the darkness of all we carry, all that is not ours and yet belongs to us.

INTO THE FIRE

The fire shoots through dry wood, crackles out a volley of hot red embers; not a fireplace, but a city under siege and burning. Yet this is a hearth, a sturdy old mantelpiece of carved oak, solid as a tree in an ancient forest. The wood suits Arthur's living room, warm with books and pottery, a space like its name, strong enough to shelter generations of the living. It feels like the only one left in the world.

On the floor is a stash of notes, my brother David's and mine. I reach for the brass screen in front of the fire, then fold it back. The flames look like teeth, a hungry row of them. No doubt they'd relish some history. I kneel down, grasp the papers, and stuff them into the burning logs. The fire lunges upward, hisses and sparks, leaving David's memory in ashes, mine as well. I am about to throw in a bundle of photos when I hear footsteps behind me, Arthur's.

"What are you burning, Donna?" he asks me.

"Junk," I tell him.

"C'mon, let me see."

Arthur grabs my wrists so that I drop the photos,

letting them fall onto the rug. He loves ancient artifacts; mine, too. On his walls are pictures: the spiral minaret of Samarra's Great Mosque, the mounds in the desert where Babylon was. And now they're torching everything, he told me last night, angry as he watched the news.

He takes both my hands and holds them, a puzzled look on his face. Younger than I am by seven years, he's happy in the company of the past, although my home town of Meredith Point, New York, is hardly a match for Troy. Neither is my history. I'm trying to be patient; Arthur's grief is complicated, as deep as mine.

"People can have too much history," I say. "Like some countries."

"Not any more," he answers.

He's been following the war in the Persian Gulf, misery enough for anyone, especially for a lover of antiquities, a student of the ancient Near East. He's been on digs there; he teaches at the University of Toronto. It terrifies him, the thought of annihilation, the death of memory. Still, these are my photos, my memories we are talking about, not humanity's and certainly not his.

"Not everything's worth saving," I answer. "Throwing out isn't the same as forgetting."

And one day you'll die, and then what, his eyes answer. Arthur lost his mother when he was young; just before her death, she couldn't remember who he was. He has spoken to me about this in the same way I talk about my brother, David, only the faint outline, like a sketch for a painting, nothing more. Now he leans over, picks up the snapshots from the carpet, and examines them carefully, as if he were prying loose a treasure from a rock.

David is running alongside me. We are twins,

eight years old, our hair and skin the colour of the beach. The curve of my foot can still feel and remember the soft fit of the sand, the shoreline of Meredith Point, how I would pretend to be a kite dancing in the air on a long string, feeling the weight of David's inner gravity pulling me back. I look at the second photo, the last I have of my brother. He's nineteen, in jeans and T-shirt, leaning against his buddy's Chev. He looks shy in front of the camera, but not unhappy, arms folded tight across his chest as if he were holding something close to him, something hidden. Slouching against the fender is his best friend, John, waving and clowning at me as I take the picture, his eyes grey and soft as ash. There's a look about him of muffled amusement, like the fizz in a pop can that would explode if you pulled the tab. I was fond of John, and the memory of him is happy. Shortly afterwards, the two of them left for Vietnam.

Arthur is looking at the photos carefully, first one, then the next. I reach over to take them from his hands.

"They're going into the fire," I tell him.

"But why?" Arthur asks. "I'll keep them if you won't."

His eyes are intent, his dark, curly hair falling around his face. At this moment he looks almost Grecian, a figure in a pantheon, the gap of a thousand years or more between us, a gap of sensitivity and grace. David and I are from the same country as the fire, destruction, the whine of bombs and rockets. Nevertheless, I'm entitled to dispose of my history if I wish.

"I will never understand what happened to David, that's why I'm doing this," I answer, trying to make sense of my feelings for him by comparing the memory of David to the ruins of Pompeii, buried airtight in volcanic rock, lava and brimstone. Centuries later archaeologists dug up, among other things, the fossilized remains of happy people eating and playing cards. And that's what it's like sifting through these photographs: I clear the devastation of war away from my mind, then ponder what it did to my brother. Yet all I have are pictures of David as I remember him, enjoying himself, running along the beach, quietly practising Mozart and Bach, helping John fix his car. There are no startled looks in these photographs, as there were on the faces of some of Pompeii's victims, there's no foreshadowing in David's eyes. The photos are ruins in the truest sense: the wreckage of what is irreparably lost. Perhaps Arthur sees this now; he puts his arm around my shoulders, carefully at first, as if I were ancient stone that might crumble at his touch.

"I'm sorry, Donna," he says. "You'd think I would have seen that." I nod slowly and gaze at the photos, then stroke them with my fingers. They feel warm where Arthur's hand was; now they carry his sorrow also. Without thinking, I take the photos and press them to my lips. A part of me still loves David; feels, as Arthur does, a need to honour the dead, to grace their lives with memory, with some affirmation of dignity and meaning. Only what happened to David had neither. Memory and destruction; Arthur and David; I am pulled between them, on a shaky bridge over a chasm. As I drop the pictures into the fire, Arthur reaches out and places his hand over mine.

"'Never that which is shall die,'" he says, quoting Euripides. It feels like a benediction as the last of the old pictures curl and blacken in the fire. I close my eyes and in the darkness feel dry wood ignite, memories crackling to life inside of me. Arthur's hands touch my skin. His fingers unearth me, remember me as I was, so that it's not the closeness of sex I feel, but the closeness of an arm or a leg to the trunk of a body, what it was like being twins. Inseparable; David's mind like a small dark seed, his memory growing in the darkness of my own.

One too many of us for our parents, burdensome; this was not even a thought, but knowledge, deep and solid, lodging in the marrow of our bones. Our parents, who were as shy as children, loved music, and it became for both of us a solace better than any of the unspoken words they might have said. Help me play the piano, I'd say to David, meaning the old, comforting one-handed way we'd practised when we were younger, a Bach bourrée; even when we were in our teens, we would sometimes do it just for fun—David playing the right hand and myself the left—and his look would soften, his shoulders relaxing into the music like a strong swimmer crawling effortlessly through waves.

Even now, I can still see his head inclined over the keyboard, resolute with inner purpose, pale as a church statue except for his eyes behind wire-rimmed glasses, a cool blue stillness in them like the heart of a flame. It was as if he could sense that music was survival in loneliness. Years later, after he got out of the army, he insisted that even as a child he could feel the music in my hands, and in them the order and beauty that Bach must have intended. He said he was not surprised I'd become a pianist, a teacher of music. By then he had given up playing.

*

Arthur is staring at the morning paper, the back page of the Arts section. He looks stunned, as he did last night when he found me burning my photographs.

"What's wrong?" I ask him.

"A little note about the Arch of Ctesiphon," he says. "It got in the way of a bomb."

"Isn't that a wreck already?" I ask. Arthur's enthusiasm for the rubble of ancient Persia makes me want to laugh sometimes, along with his fretting over the destruction of what is already dead. Rather than hurt his feelings, I nod with the deference of a schoolchild taken to pray in a darkened cathedral, all the while knowing that Arthur hasn't even heard my question. He's already perusing the bookshelf, pulling out tomes, catalogues of his digs, flipping through the pages of diagrams and photos.

"The arch really has presence," he says. "Pictures give you some idea of it, here, have a look."

The photo is one he took on the east bank of the Tigris River: what remains of the central hall of a sixth-century Persian palace. It is not at all beautiful, with an inner wall of brick and mortar, its pale surface rough and blotchy like diseased skin. The vaulted ceiling has a huge, ragged hole torn out of it, foreshadowing its complete destruction. The damage makes it look uncentred, off balance. It's a miracle of engineering that it has stood.

"What happened?" I ask Arthur, pointing to the hole.

"Empires come and go," he says. "Time did a little dance on the roof."

I look again at the broken arch and notice the ancient grace of this vaulted ceiling, its imperfection and its massive strength, and its roughness intrigues me, as if its art were in its brokenness, its survival of humankind. Then Arthur lifts the photo out of its plastic envelope, slips it in his breast pocket, and asks me if I'd like to come along to a peace march. That's not his usual style or mine, but he explains that this is a professional commitment, a chance to bear witness on behalf of ancient ruins. We would be silent, dignified; no shouting of slogans, no waving placards.

The past is a human voice talking in Arthur; it is everywhere around him, calm as light falling through the leaves of trees; in me it shouts, buried alive, pounding its fists to get out. That's what has come of burning pictures, papers; memory is outraged; it's a fault line shifting underground, an angry rumble deep in the earth. Instinct tells me this will not be a march but a small excavation; my feet will scrape the dust off memories as I walk, and I'm afraid.

*

"Steel drums," Arthur says. He's spotted two guys lugging a huge metal drum, bumping and banging it through the crowd like pedlars selling wares. I tell him no.

"It's an oil drum; you have to cut the bottom off for music," I answer. Arthur starts to laugh. He'd never thought of music; he was simply puzzled at the sight of this enormous black drum, two guys clunking it along the west side of University Avenue, disappearing into the stream of bodies that are moving and swirling around us like tendrils of long hair on the waters of the sea. It's as if someone were drowning, the waves of the ocean pulling us into an undertow. I don't like this; I feel afraid of the pulse of energy; but Arthur takes my hand as we join the line of marchers trudging back and forth in front of the U.S. consulate. Arthur walks silently, head bowed. At times he touches his breast pocket where he keeps his photo of the arch. We are surrounded by placards mounted on tall poles, moving and shifting like the sails and masts of a giant ship listing forward and back. I feel as if I'm rocking on the swells, growing dizzy, when I hear a shout, a rhythmic clapping, someone yelling *hell no, we won't go*, and then the whole chain of bodies in front of us and behind starts shouting, swaying back and forth, in and out to the rhythmic chant, like the segments of a giant earthworm, a snake being charmed.

Arthur squeezes my hand. Neither of us joins in the chant; we just keep walking back and forth, pacing like lions in cages; I feel trapped. Now someone is in front of me with a megaphone, shouting right in my face, *no blood for oil,* trying to get all of us screaming. I'm sure she's aiming her clenched fist at me, as if I'm the one who's shedding blood; as if she can see David's stride in my long legs, his anger in my clenched fists. David in me wants to fire a gun, choke this woman with a necklace of bullets. My hands cover my face; Arthur pulls me aside.

"Are you okay?" he asks me.

"I feel David here," I answer. I know that my brother is watching this scene from behind my eyes, as if their sockets were huge grottoes, sandbagged emplacements. He's tunnelling into the hardening lines of my face, crouched in ambush, ready to strike, his old war stuck inside this new one like a lump of food caught in the throat, choking off air. Arthur puts his arm around my shoulder.

"It's all right; we can go home," he says. I shake my head. There's no point in my leaving; David will only follow me. I don't mind marching on behalf of falling brick and masonry; we are the echo of its silence here; it's a reminder of our dignity. Arthur touches his pocket once again; his thoughts move like air through palace walls, through the lost city of Ctesiphon.

"It's like opening a graveyard, destroying a ruin from the air," he says. "Thunder of the gods driving out the spirits."

"When you're a twin," I say, "you get used to being haunted."

"Is that how you're feeling now?" he asks me.

Yes, I answer. Haunted; a human dig. I start to laugh.

"What's funny?" Arthur asks.

"If I were a ruin, which one would I be?"

"Petra, the City of Tombs," he says. "Strange and lovely; carved of sandstone, out of the rock cliffs. They called it the rose-red city once, more like a beautiful opal in the desert."

"And very dead," I answer.

"The Romans didn't think so," says Arthur. "They built their amphitheatre in the ancient tombs; they performed among the dead. I think they were at peace with that."

This feels consoling, pondering the beauties and shadows of the distant past; we become like ghosts ourselves, invisible in the line of marchers, our voices low against the shouting that grates on the ears like static, like a radio station badly tuned. Two hikers on a thousand-year journey, my backpack full of memories; I see David once again, going camping with his friend John, saying his pack was as heavy as any soldier's. David carried much, but not lightly, not without images of struggle and pain. The thought comes into my mind like rain through an open window: David also carried me. I was his twin, a line of music, the other half of everything he played. David was too brittle a vessel to hold the weight of my kinship; he had not gotten over our parents' silence; I didn't help him enough; excuses. David had his limits, as I have; this is the burden he did not carry well.

Arthur leans over and adjusts my backpack, which is starting to slip from my shoulder. Since the war began, I remember my brother and fill my pack with music, with all that's left of our higher aspirations: written notes strung together, ropes of light like stars that give us direction and in whose beauty we may one day divine our hidden purpose. Unlike David, I have promised myself I will do no harm; I will keep walking right here, feet on the ground, until he is no longer in me. Ancient ruins; gripping a shovel, I will drive it into hard, compacted earth, loosening roots, turning over stones.

*

"Those guys with the drums are back," Arthur says. I can hear the clanking: two men rolling that metal barrel down the street, black with the word OIL painted on in white. Arthur wants to know what's going on here; his eyes pick through the faces in the crowd as if they were a collection of facts, only a few of them worthy of notice. He's spotted a colleague from his department and he wants to talk to him; maybe this professor has heard some scant report about the ruins along the Tigris, which ones have survived bombardment and which have not. I continue walking back and forth under the swaying placards; I glance down at my new running shoes, white ones, blue racing stripes like ocean waves curling up along the sides. They remind me of the seashore, summer at Meredith Point, of a beach of fine sand, of rock crumbling into the whiteness of dust.

*

(The night before David and John left, we went to the beach with our friends, partying under the black sky, the waves flipping the moon back and forth like a silver coin; heads you'll live through Vietnam, tails you won't. David smiled at me, but his eyes were sombre; he was breathing in my thoughts. John was more relaxed and nonchalant, acting smart like an older brother, but he was only two years older. Not to worry, kid, he said, his hidden laughter fizzing inside, and I remember dancing with him on the beach, whirling with excitement like an eddy of sand in the wind. Later John wrote from Vietnam, and he told me what a great time he'd had with me that night; how he'd be back for that big fat moon bouncing along the waves, like the Guy Up There was dribbling a basketball, just getting ready to score.

A year later, John was dead, killed in an ambush. David wrote to tell me this, his pen skidding on ice-cold words.)

*

I move through the crowd of marchers, trying to locate

Arthur, only now it's impossible to make my way across the sidewalk; there are great brown padded lumps, human sandbags underfoot, a bizarre scale-model desert terrain. I'm picking my way along the curb on University Avenue in front of the U.S. consulate, trying not to step on the pretend-dead in down-filled body-bags, trying not to shove or be pushed, not to tumble down, backpack and all, on top of the heap.

David has come back, I can feel him in me watching, feel my throat tightening like a fist, choking on what I can't swallow; and then memory grabs me from behind like the huge slap of a wave, throwing me face down in the water, washing me like flotsam to the shore, then yanking me into the undertow again, back into David inside the glassy water, lost and floating away like a twist of seaweed in the pull of the tide. David came home from the war, but drifted away from us; he wouldn't say what hurt him most. The polished ebony lid on the baby grand made him think of open caskets; he wouldn't return to his music. I can't imagine what you've been through, I said, hoping he'd talk, but he was beyond talk, on the opposite side of a chasm. His body was full of the knowledge of death, of fear as strong as a wild animal's scent.

He moved out of town and rented himself a room; I asked if I could help him fix it up, and he was touched, as if I were giving him a gift he neither expected nor deserved. While we worked, I happen to mention how sorry I was about John, and how much I'd liked him. David stopped to listen and I could feel him inside my thoughts, parting the tangle of memory like a scout who is desperate to find his way home through the underbrush. Then he shook his head, his blue eyes deep with resignation and sorrow. John, he whispered, and he sat with his face in his hands, as if he'd somehow caused my pain and his.

That's why I feel David's eyes, not mine, watching the scene before me, which is like battle, the cold memory of what he held inside pressing at the back of my head like the steel of a gun held there. Two hundred people are blocking one lane of traffic on University Avenue, rolling those huge empty oil drums into the street, banging on the sides and shouting *no blood for oil.* I'm having a hard time edging my way along the curb, trying to spot Arthur, who's vanished into the crowd. When I get to the corner, I see those two big guys blocking off the crosswalk, setting an oil drum in the middle of the lane, right side up; they light a match and drop it straight down. What have they poured into it? Maybe a few drops of gasoline, all they need for a giant whoosh, an explosion, flame, a huge cheer. People are applauding, linking hands, dancing around the fire that is crackling and hissing, lightning-yellow along the edges of the drum. They are chanting and clapping: *U.S.A. get lost, oil isn't worth a holocaust,* and now I can see David walking through his own fire, and I can hear the screams he heard under the thatched roofs in Vietnam, straw igniting, exploding into a yellow-fisted ball of gas; now I'm remembering for him how they torched a village: people running out of huts, black rags of clothes fluttering off their bodies like the tattered wings of small, wounded birds.

And David, my brother who loved to play Mozart and Bach, whose eyes lit like a calm, still flame as he sat at the piano, whose hands lifted music out of the keys as gently as you might lift a child from a cradle; that man, my brother, said to me, I grabbed my fucking rifle and shot them all dead but for one girl hiding in the bushes, the only one in the village left alive; and he was about to show me how he drew his bayonet, only now he's crying, all ready to tell me about the touch of his hands on her neck and what he went and did to her, and I can hear myself screaming at him, shut up, David, I don't want to hear about this.

And now I can hear him in the crackle of flame; feel inside and around me the war that floods the embankments of the earth, whose fires they will never put out, this terror there is no beginning of nor end to; this image of my brother lying face up on his bed, trails of blood from a gunshot wound spreading over his body like the tributaries of a dark river, the fingers of a hand. And now I know I have no history worth saving, none. Memory strikes rock and stops here, and I stare down into the grave that is opening up under our feet, the pit we have dug for ourselves, the ruin of everything.

I turn my eyes away, see Arthur's body zigzag through the crowd, part of a human chain. His face is pale and angry. He's with that professor and a few other men and women, striding up to the guys who set fire to the oil drums, shoving the crowd of chanting people aside, and I can hear them shouting so that their voices rise over the singsong, crisp and hot as flame: you could kill someone, put that damn thing out. A blue knot of cops moves in: I overhear one of them telling Arthur, we'll handle this, and that's when he turns around and sees me.

The anger slides away from his face like sheet-ice in sunlight, and he looks at me with sorrow and regret. Then he walks over and puts his arms around me. After a minute Arthur lets go, and then, very gently, he places his hands on my face, tilting it slightly towards him. His eyes are full of awe and compassion, as if he were uncovering more than a gift, memory etched in an ancient frieze, ineffable beauty that was not of me. I am crying.

"I was with David in the fire," I say. "'God doesn't forgive everything,' that's what he told me."

David left a note; he wrote those words. Arthur knows this and now his hands do also; their touch moves across the contours of my cheeks like light over valleys, still in the late day's passing from the earth. He is afraid of breaking something; I can feel at the tips of his fingers the delicacy of my own skin, and the frail human clay that is his. He brushes his lips against my forehead, almost reverently.

"I am grateful for your life," he says, as we move through this desert, feeling around us the white dust of ruined cities.

HOW, IF EVER, THE STORY ENDS

Prologue, January 1991

This is about remembering, about Donna who is a musician, and about her brother, David, who asked her to burn
these papers. It never occurred to her to honour his wishes,
not until now. Instead, she did the opposite. She stored
their notes and letters in a white giftbox, sealing the lid
with electrical tape as if it were edged with frayed wires that
might short and spark. For years the box sat in the crawl-
space, hidden under blankets and pillows, along with a
manila envelope of photographs and a sheaf of David's old
music scores, his name written on each of them in a fine,
meticulous hand. Donna had her own copies of this
music, Mozart, Schubert, Bach. When she left New York
for Toronto, she took David's sheaf with her, felt its
closeness like a ghostly amputated limb, a memory of her
twin who'd once loved music.

   Donna saved the writing, even though she'd come
to feel uneasy about words, the way they seemed to trap
what music freed. Time, memory, and spirit, bound and

gagged in books, sealed in boxes; that's what history felt like. Yet she had no choice; she had to write. David had fought in Vietnam, filling Donna with his nightmares and her own premonitions, images that needed language to cast them out of her body as you might cast out a devil with a blessing. Words had blessed her; maybe this was why she saved them.

In the box she swept up these writings like shards of broken glass into a dustpan. It was 1969 and David had come home. Eventually, the war killed him or he killed himself, depending on how you told the story. Here we have to pause for the benefit of sceptics who will remind us that this happened in the sixties, back when men were men and stories were stories, beginning, middle, and end, their freight derailed only by bad trips or a few dime bags of Acapulco Gold. Do Not Deconstruct, the sign reads. After all, what has been left standing? David killed himself; his story's over.

No, Donna says. She doesn't think of endings, but of transformations, of the endless loop of matter into energy. She imagines flame hissing at the top of a match, notes of lightning at the tips of her fingers. Fire, kinetic as music, both of them leaping into the dry tinder where language fails, where the story changes form and lives.

This is about stories and how we tell them, how we give them endings, and how, if ever, the story ends. How we tell them: Donna felt that fragments were appropriate, not the preserving of memory, its civilized mellowing from grapes to wine, no, nothing like that. Bits of life shaken loose; transcripts of tapes, excerpts from letters and notes, journals she'd written like stories; stories she'd invented, all of it patched together so that the words might reveal whatever truth they could. Letters back and forth from Vietnam; not correspondence; shards of flying glass. Donna picked each of them out of her skin, then set these fragments down.

About endings, and how, if ever, the story ends: nothing ends. The Persian Gulf war is on television; Babylon laid waste, David's war come to life in fire. Donna thinks of this as she opens the grate and strikes a match to wood. As it sparks and crackles into flame, she rips the tape off the box, removes the lid, pulls out the papers, and begins to read. This is how she remembers: she will set loose a fire on the world.

*

Vietnam/Oct. 1967–Feb. 1968
Found Poem/Excerpts from David's letters

At night I sleep like a tree cut down dead.

*

Dream you're marching with me, Donna.
"Look out!" I yell at you before the mine goes off,
only it's me flying out of my skin.
A real twin-dream.

*

John says wish you were here, bring your piano when you come.
Bach's Concerto in D would give this place class.

John says he loves you. When he's stoned, he makes up songs,
screams them out to the jungle,
strange words, they all sound like your name.

*

Dead eyes before they shut, they crack like mirrors.
You see your broken face in them.
I should be used to that,
being a twin.

*

feel shame almost never
feel tired always
miss you

Meredith Point, N.Y./Fall 1967
Excerpts from Donna's letters to David

I'm practising a difficult passage from Chopin. You're in
my hands on the notes, a real twin-thing. I feel underbrush
and rifles, I play a polonaise, the notes are you marching.

*

. . . John and I were dancing, a beach party, low tide, full
moon, stars like small change falling from pockets. Hard
to imagine how he'll camouflage that look of his, bright as
silver. Tell him to be careful.

—115—

*

Now here's a twin-dream, I wasn't sure whether to send it, but you've asked for these.

I'm in battle fatigues, a feeling of menace, someone about to jump me from behind. I turn around, take aim, see it's you, David. What are you doing here, I ask. You shake your head and vanish. I keep marching, and as I march, the rays of the sun gather in my body, draw together light and heat, so that I become the lens of an eye, a gun-sight, a burning halo, a fire to a village in a valley below me where I'm falling downward into the skin of a man in battle fatigues covered with mud. I look out from behind his eyes, seeing the two cracked halves of a woman's face, as if I were trying to focus her image in the viewfinder of a camera, but I can't. She's screaming, as if I'd wounded her with the crack in my field of vision. I pick up my rifle and take aim, not really sure why I'm doing this, and then I become myself again. You're the man holding the rifle, you put it down when I call your name but you're blinded; when I touch you, you don't know who I am.

*

Vietnam/1 March 1968 (barely legible)

Donna:
John died, killed in an ambush on the road to [illegible place-name] happened quick [line crossed out]. The guy loved you. I'm sorry I have to tell you this.

David

*

Meredith Point, N.Y., April 1968/Donna (excerpt)

Poor John.
I never knew him as well as you did. I'm trying to play him
into my music, trying not to give up hope.

*

Vietnam, Summer 1968/David (excerpts)

A sergeant comes riding by in a jeep, his antenna strung
with ears. Come and get it, fresh today, he says. I laughed
my fucking head off. Later I thought of Beethoven going
deaf. Wanted to cry and couldn't.
  It gets worse, Donna. Don't ask how.
  Just no shame in these hands. No music left.

*

Thank God for grass, God who if he's there must weep.

*

Donna's journal, 17 June 1969

David doesn't notice me at first. He comes through the
gate, then glances up at the big shuttered house. There is
a flag to welcome him; crimson and white, its stars jabbed
into the blue field. The veranda is sedate with wicker
chairs, pink geraniums, an ice bucket full of beer, a table

set for lunch. Only David is watching this as if it were TV. His hand wants to reach out for the fine-tuning knob that will bring this homey picture into the real world, his world. Now his eyes are resting on a flowering dogwood, his hands touching the fleshy petals, their tips crusty and red like dried blood. I call out his name, run down the steps and hug him. He looks startled.

"It's just me, David."

"Sis," he says, and puts his arms around me. I'm crying. It's two years he's been overseas. His uniform is the dull sand colour of the beach.

"You been sick, Donna?" he asks. Mother must have written him. I nod yes and dry my eyes.

"I'm sorry for crying. I get like this."

"No, don't be sorry." Neither of us is in mint condition; that's what his eyes say. They are like mine, a blue that reminds me of mother's delicate china, the plates woven with cracks from the tiny, indifferent cuts of forks and knives. Already we have seen too much; this is how one pair of eyes greets the other. Twins. Twenty-one years old, and we have grown tired of seeing.

"Let me take your bag," I say. David shakes his head no, grips it, strides forward, his back straight. I slip behind his eyes and into his body, see what he sees, a jungle, a dangerous, restful green where death hides, crouched and waiting. The fingers of my hands curl like the roots and tendrils of a dead plant, grip hard to the steel of a rifle. I shake myself free of this.

"David, you look tired." More than this, he looks exhausted, ravaged. Pain has scored his face like a knife in meat. Pain opens you, his eyes say. The same way a surgeon opens you. He puts his bag down.

"Are you well, David?" He pauses.

"Tired. They sent me home."

"I dreamt you were coming. I saw you pack your bags."

"I dreamt you playing Bach. Whenever I slept, I dreamt you."

Donna's journal, 18 June 1969

Mother's meeting Dad for supper at the golf club, but David and I have taken a rain check. Just as she's about to leave, the phone rings. My brother answers it.

"Son-of-a-gun, you're back!" The voice of an old neighbour, Mr. Williams. "How the hell was Kathmandu?"

Silence.

"Vietnam."

"You went backpacking in Vietnam? Friggin' war on."

"I was in the army." Mother grabs the receiver from David's hand and asks us both to leave the room. Our eyes share puzzled glances. David and John once talked a lot about going to Nepal, and Mr. Williams, on business much of the time in Europe, has simply not heard otherwise. When she gets off the phone, she apologizes to both of us.

"You never clued him in?" David asks.

"I don't see him often," she says. "I hate to trouble people with the war."

"That's where I was. Real bullets."

"Mr. Williams has a heart condition."

Mother's rattled. She leaves for the club and I pour my brother a drink.

"Don't be upset with her," I tell him. "She's worried about us both. It's my fault she's a wreck." David looks troubled.

"What happened, Donna?"

"I kind of had a breakdown. Broke up with a guy."

"You all right?"

"I'll tell you about it."

"Mother wrote, said you had mono." David grimaces, pours me a drink. "You, mono. Me, Kathmandu."

"She didn't want to worry you, David, I'm sure of it."

(Only we both know better, know about her white lies, how they hint at so much pain, trouble she can't bear to touch. She wants to soften the world for us, knead it into pleasing shapes, dangle them before our eyes like those huge baubles that make a baby laugh. Part of me wants to be seduced by this and I wonder if *I'm* telling tales, if I know what's true, what really happened. Maybe I never met Larry the soldier or had a breakdown, moving through his body and into the terror of seeing where you were. David, maybe I only imagined you went to Vietnam, came back yesterday, a map of pain on your face, the sick kind of map that helps you lose your way. Mother is quiet, as if she sees nothing. Maybe nothing happens worth seeing. I feel confused, incredibly tired.)

"Here's to the truth," David says. "*In vino veritas.*"

I lift my glass.

Notes, 25 June 1969/David

I shot them all dead.

This girl, I held a bayonet to her neck and laughed. Every night this week, the same dream: I'm on top of her, giving her one for John. I wake up crying.

*

Donna's story, Part I (30 June 1969)

Here is the only way I can talk about what happened last summer, when I broke down. The story is fiction. Truth is its pulse, the blood in its veins. Language could never describe what really happened.

WAR STORY

Here's a riddle, a woman named Heather who came to the island for the privacy of mist and damp, as if she were naked and this were a curtain she could draw around her body. What are we to make of her? She took a room in a narrow old white frame house on a sloping street full of dogwood and trailing ailanthus, the street running straight downhill to the harbour. Heather had no family. She was a musician, but she didn't earn her living at it, not yet. For summer work, she followed the road uphill a mile, making the right turn that took her to a U.S. army base, Fort Travis, to an office job full of paper, silence.

There was a grand piano in the auditorium at the base, and Heather asked permission to practise during lunch hour. One afternoon, a Chopin étude drew in a soldier who sat down to listen in the back of the hall. Before she'd finished, he left. Every day that week he returned, each time advancing a few rows. Heather let the music in her hands draw him, as if he were an undersea creature snagged in a net that swept the darkness of the ocean floor. By the end of the week, the soldier was sitting in the front row.

"Real nice music," he said to her, introducing himself as Bill. He was a dark-haired man with kind, pensive eyes. His parents were musicians. Soon he'd be shipping out to Vietnam, and he'd come to feel her playing was a talisman, one that could shield him from harm. Bill took Heather for a walk, then a drink. He told her he was married. She said she'd come here for the summer, for the quiet.

You'd think she'd know better than to get involved. Hadn't she wanted to be invisible? Maybe she was. Maybe her body could find pleasure in someone's bed while the rest of her floated upward like warm air rising, away from trouble, impervious to harm. Maybe this was why she had come here, in order to be invisible, to know the unseen. Bill took her to a run-down hotel, to a room that reeked of cheap perfume and disinfectant. Heather smelled a far-off hospital, saw this bed open up into a grave, a bend in time where Bill had fallen into the moment of his death. She found herself drawn to these foreshadowings, this undertow of a hidden sea.

Each time they made love, Heather saw details—flying shrapnel, his stepping on a mine—until her knowledge became an affliction. She would feel her hands moving across his body like a clock's, drawing him closer to the hour and minute of his death. Bill would come inside her, crying out, as if from the place where he was going to die.

Mornings before work, she'd look for relief from

the night before, walking to the docks, listening for the eddies of water, the sound of them lapping against the rough wooden pier, its quick, dark contours softened in the mist. Soldiers stood waiting there with duffel bags, fog and cigarette smoke curling around them, grey and soft as the tails of alley cats. And then one day, barely awake, she stumbled into the moment, still invisible, yet here: Bill watching for a troop ship, its prow slicing knife-like through the fog, its maw opening to swallow him. Heather began to feel what she wanted least: the shape of his body moulded into hers, the indelible mark of it, like thumb-prints in clay. Everything was pressing into her with the force of his body: the dock, the harbour, sky and water like a huge eye milky with cataracts and slowly going blind.

(To Be Continued)

Donna's journal, 5 July 1969

. . . I also recall Mother reading one of David's letters, her back to me, crying, and how even here I felt time folding, then into now, like a pleat in cloth, so that mother was twenty years old, reading the telegram that shot her older brother down from the British sky. When I tried to comfort her, she composed herself and told me everything was fine, really. Then what was the undertow I'd felt, the tug of energy? She said it was nothing.

"Afraid she might crack, that's why she froze like that," David said. "A real soldier."

"Couldn't she talk to me?"

"She'd come apart, Donna."

"Dad wouldn't talk much either. He followed Vietnam in *The Wall Street Journal.*" David looked at me, his eyes sad.

"I'm starting to know how they got that way," he said.

"How?"

David lowered his eyes. "Got scared," he answered. "Looked inside. Found out who they are."

David's notes, 10 July 1969

. . . sat on the edge of gut-shitting panic, felt my body bend and fall into the slow way time has of moving when you're scared and hold your breath, a heavy step behind me and I jumped, spun around, my hand hard, a steel blade, a knife held flat, a clean slip between the ribs, I'm ready. Eyes of a panther glinting, VC moving through underbrush like a cold slit of moon coming through night and I was all set to jump him when two hands clamped themselves over my arms, then pushed me back down on the bed.

"David, for chrissakes," Dad said. He sat down next to me, and now I was shaking, not sure where the hell I was.

"Thought I was a goner," I told him.

"I know," he said. "I saw your eyes."

I looked at him, his face like mine only older, the pain dredged right in, like trenches in a battlefield. My dad never talked about his war. No words, but his whole fucking body knew what I saw, I was sure it did because I could feel his thoughts like they were prisoners behind enemy lines, locked up all these years in the *Wall Street Journal*, the boardroom, the dead-cold silence. Now both of us were prisoners of war, both of us knowing you couldn't talk about what happened, words were invented

—124—

by civilized people, there were no damn words left. We were looking at each other through iron bars, his and mine.

"Promise you'll get some rest," dad said. "Your mind's playing tricks."

I promised.

*

Donna's journal, 15 July 1969

Groves Island, forty miles away, that's where David's moving. I know the place; I worked there last summer, a sea-weathered town, an island that felt like a ghostly barge that at any time might shrug us off, pack itself up, and float away into the mist. The place had its own life, indifferent to ours; an inner stillness. This is what David wants, along with a simple job that will leave him time to think and to sort out his life. Mother and Dad are worried about him leaving. They think he needs help, but he says he's not crazy enough, not yet.

"I'll miss you," I said. I felt like crying. I remembered the docks creaking with their loads of duffel bags and soldiers bounding off the ferry like dice rolling from the hands of a croupier. The chances you take, I thought to myself.

"You're remembering Larry," David said. I told him I was. My brother's eyes were full of compassion.

"Neither of us is much for talking, are we?"

"We always had music," I said. David would no longer play the piano, and now we had to find words, to invent the language we'd never had. I told him I'd come out to Groves Island for a few weeks. Maybe we'd unearth the words, dredge them up from the sea like sunken cargo, away from the storms in our parents' lives that had drowned them long ago.

"You'll feel better, Donna."

"I've got the war in my veins, like you." David looked puzzled.

"Here now, you be happy, kid," he said. "You haven't hurt anyone."

He rolled a joint, lit it, and we passed it back and forth until we both felt comforted.

*

Donna's story, Part II, 18 July 1969

WAR STORY
(Continued)

Bill and Heather would sit at the hotel bar talking music. He'd have a few drinks, and then he'd start in on Vietnam and shipping out, his tongue heavy under the words. The ice in his glass would rattle from the shake of his hand, a cold, tight static, as if the war were an electrical current running along the nerves and tendons of his arm, shooting right into his fingers. Later they'd smoke grass in their room. Bill would calm down, and Heather would forget her premonition that Bill was going to die. She'd drift through sex like a boat becalmed in fog, sinking into the dark peace of the water.

One evening, a guy named Mike joined them for drinks, a congenial-looking soldier who was dealing grass. They left the bar, went upstairs, and rolled a few together.

"They got this stuff in Nam, I'll deal," Mike said.

"I'll buy," Bill answered. "Get the shit blown out of me, toked up."

"Cool it, man, you fuckin' depress me." Mike looked at Bill, then at Heather, in a way that made her uneasy.

"Let's show your man a good time," he said. She turned to Bill. He shrugged, lowered his eyes.

"'s okay, go on. Pretend he's me."

Heather didn't move. Bill sat up and put his hands on her shoulders.

"Hey, kid, we're all pals," he said. "Let's love each other while we got it, huh?" Bill reached over, undid Heather's dress, pulled it off, then eased her back on the bed. She let him, her muscles limp as string. Mike slipped inside her, came as quickly as turning out a light.

Heather blacked out, and then it seemed it was happening all over again, the pleasure more intense this time. Either that or she was dreaming Bill, the feel of his tongue slipping in and out of her mouth as a wave slithers into a narrow cove, leaving behind the salt taste of his words, I want you, I'm going to die.

On the sea becalmed, she heard the soft moan of a foghorn, heard her own voice crying at the fuzzy halo of a lighthouse beam. She opened her eyes in time to see Mike leaving the room, Bill beside her, weeping.

(To Be Continued)

Letter to Groves Island, 21 July 1969

Dear David,
. . . There are so many ways to tell a story. Let's try to share the past two years, however we can.

I feel words banging around inside me, pictures of the war; I've got to let them out. You must feel this also. I'm writing a story I will let you read.

Now that you're settled on the island, I'll come to visit. Have you got a phone yet?

Donna

Tape Transcript #1, 24 July 1969

Recorded in David's room, 107 Washington St., Groves Island, N.Y. We have decided to speak to each other about the war, to share whatever we can of the past two years, both in conversation and in writing. I will be spending the summer with a friend on the island, studying music and giving some shape to these recollections.

(Later note) The tapes were made with the built-in microphone on my cassette recorder. I set it up a few feet away from us so that we wouldn't be distracted or inhibited. As a result, the sound quality isn't the best. There's a lot of chair scraping, foot shuffling, etc.—one reason for doing these transcriptions.

David:	Didn't know you were going to record this.
Donna:	It's an idea I had, to get the sound of our voices, the emotion. Like notes of music. The real story of Vietnam, our version.
David:	Good luck.

Donna: Do you want to start?

David: Okay, sure. You asked me why the hell I let them ship me off to Vietnam, well, I didn't pick a war, they sent me. Thought about staying in college, all of five minutes. *(pause)* I guess I wanted company, guys, something I didn't have to share with you. Being your twin, you were clothes I was wearing. Felt I was inside your fingers. Couldn't find me. *(laughs)*

Donna: You could have said something. It might have saved you a war.

David: Yeah, maybe. John kept me sane. Him and music, drumming in the garage, he played riffs on my car when I took it in for a tune-up. He was a real musician, sound came rolling right off him. Same as you.

Donna: And you.

David: *(pause)* Fuck it, no. I don't do music now.

Donna: *(off-mike)* Wherever you are, John, how about a drum roll? David needs a wake-up call.

David: Knock it off, Donna.

Donna: What's the matter?

David: Let's forget about John, huh?

Donna: He was a friend of ours. I don't want to forget about him. Neither do you, if you're honest.

David: *(pause)* I'm sorry, I take it back.

Donna: You were going to talk about how we met him.

David: It was at a jazz concert, John on drums, yeah, I remember how his whole body drummed. He had his eye on you the whole time. Then he took us out drinking. Said he'd show us how to blow scales on beer bottles. So he lined up

a row of them, a little bit of suds in each one, then he played "Oh, Donna", oh-Do-on-na, oh-Don-na, tooting it out in the key of C. The guy had perfect pitch.

Donna: He said it was in E Major. Four sharps. What a showoff. *(pause)* Something wrong, David?

David: *(barely audible)* Just remembering a trip we took once.

Donna: Tell me.

David: *(pause)* Fucking miss John, is all I can tell you. *(Muffled sound for much of the above. David's notes continue the story).*

David's journal, 24 July 1969/addressed to Donna

. . . So this one weekend the two of us, me and John, we went camping in the Catskills, pitched a tent, and built a fire. After we ate, I sat there poking at the embers, little chunks of light spitting through the ash and floating up to the stars, and then it hit me, Jesus, how alone I felt, and how I wanted the craziest thing, just to put a hand on his shoulder.

Scared? Hell, I couldn't let the feeling move from the knot in my chest to the place in the mind where all the right words come. So I said to John the first thing that came to my head: you ever think of running away? He paused, said how do you mean? Running away, just that, I answered. Disappear, melt like snow, not a damn trace of you. John put a hand on my shoulder, said you working too hard, pal, or what?

So we started talking, me about music, my family, the pressure I felt that I had to be Vladimir Fucking

Horowitz; about Mother and Dad, the way they'd look distracted when we talked to them, like they were at a cocktail party, ready to flit off to the next conversation, except they weren't much for talking. John was a good guy; he listened. Turned out that's all I'd wanted, just to have him listen.

No more now, Donna. When I think of what happened to John, I feel my body turn into a fist, stone-hard. Can't talk, can't write, can't hold a pen. I'm sorry.

*

Donna's journal, 29 July 1969

David has taken a job as a janitor in the small apartment building near the waterfront where he lives. He likes the simple and orderly routine, the attention he must pay to human need, to silence and reflection. The place he's rented is clean and spare: a cot, a chair and table, a ceiling lamp, a tiny kitchenette, a few cheerful posters he's put on the walls. Jimi Hendrix, Richie Havens, John and Yoko in bed for peace; another with psychedelic flourishes, an art-deco lady with long, curling locks and a pipe, the smoke from it forming the words God Grows His Own. Beethoven's up there, too; my gift, David's old, neglected friend. He thanked me.

Seeing his setup, it's hard to believe that, not so long ago, David was a soldier. Or maybe he's what soldiers look like now, a sturdy, well-built man, but otherwise not so very different from the rest of us, the way he flaunts his ragged denims with the peace sign stitched on the leg, a red printed headband, his old white T-shirt bearing the face of

Martin Luther King, an army jacket with the bars and brass ripped off. Except that my brother feels like a refugee, dressed in the kind of leftover clothing that churches collect for the poor. He is not a flower-child, not at peace. He sits before me and drinks the tea I've made him, but today his face looks so stricken that even when I close my eyes, I can't blot out the desolate look of it, his features chiselled as if his face were stone and someone had taken a knife to him.

"Are you okay, David?" I asked. He rolled a joint, lit up, inhaled, passed it to me.

"I'm dreaming a lot. A woman sits on the window-sill," he said. "Like a bird, just flies here."

"What's her name?"

"Don't know. Every night I see her. A bruise on her throat blooming like a flower, a purple orchid."

"Poor thing."

David paused, his throat tight. "I love her. Every night I dream I get her into bed."

"You're lonesome, David. I know some nice girls, I'll introduce you."

He smiled a little. "She's the one I want."

"David, how much of that stuff are you smoking?" I felt scared.

"Enough to help me get some sleep."

He looked at me through the sweet and pungent haze. His face, his eyes, a thousand tiny cracks in them, the ceramic look of parched and desolate earth where nothing will grow, as if every trouble were a vast and spreading desert of human grief, one that didn't begin or end with him. And here I was, sure that talk would help, stories. The hope seemed as frail as my brother.

"You should see a doctor if you can't sleep."

"I've thought of it. Only they'd never believe me about the girl."

"David, I'm worried about you."

It took a minute for my words to register. When they did, my brother put a hand on my arm. His touch was almost too light, as if touch were new to him, unsure as he was of kindness, of how the hands show it.

"Don't want you worrying. Two years I had you worried."

He finished the joint, then looked away, his eyes scanning the Beatles posters, the psychedelic art, the table where we sat by the window, looking down the street at a waterfront bar, a dive as crummy as they come, its pink and green neon sign blinking GIRLS GIRLS GIRLS. Tacked to the windowframe was a small photo of a man in uniform: John. David's eyes stopped there. I poured him more tea.

"I miss him too, David."

"I fucking loved John." At the hotel across the street, there were hookers standing in the doorways.

"What if I bring you curtains for these windows?"

David looked relieved and thanked me.

*

David's notes, 1 August 1969

After work, toked up, taking a walk on the docks somewhere in Asia, South China Sea. A big smudge of Chinese neon, drizzling rain, the city's a big eye trying to cry me out of it. Where the hell am I, what country, soldiers in pedicabs, no. Hippies, bad trippers, tie-dyed runaways, lonely people, artists from the beach end of the island; this girl on the docks with a head of long black hair that she shakes and tosses like a tambourine, maybe I'm supposed to hear music, see glints of light sparking off her. She wears a corsage, a clump of purple violets. I touch her arm, let her walk into a gut-lonely place inside me where she asks what I want and I ask her how much and then it doesn't matter once she does it, at least that's how I tell the story now.

Then when I want her name, she says no, they all want her name, she's a mass grave, dead and wounded in the hollow between her legs. Her eyes talk: pay me in seeds of blood, let them explode into blue-black roses on your throat, then I won't have to tell you my name; you'll know who I am, you'll know.

Scared, I see cracks in her eyes, hear John screaming, falling dead in the street below. I tell her I don't need her name. I get out fast. I swear this happened.

*

Tape Transcript #2, 5 August 1969

Donna: You said you wanted to talk some more about John.

David: John's why I feel crazy sometimes. The other night walking home, heard him screaming, like they'd just shot him dead. His eyes were mirrors with cracks in them, dead eyes. I fell through them, into the war, into another city by the South China Sea, only here.

Donna:	The war is bleeding into everything.
David:	Don't follow.
Donna:	Like that time when Mother was reading your mail. She was getting the news of her brother shot down. Time just folded in on itself. It's the same with you. You fell through a hole in the world.
David:	John keeps dying, over and over.
Donna:	I understand, I miss him too. We slept together once, I guess you know that.
David:	Yeah, no secrets in the army.
Donna:	It never went further. Maybe it was just as well. Mother and Dad were upset that I liked him. Maybe they thought we'd end up working in his garage.
David:	They should see me now, mopping floors. *(pause)* Thought you were in love with John.
Donna:	No, David, I wasn't.
David:	Should have asked you first. Didn't want to share him with you, he was my best friend. Talked him out of going back to school.
Donna:	So you both got drafted.
David:	I was an idiot. *(long silence)*
Donna:	It's not your fault he died.
David:	Right in front of me, he got shot, like I drop down and he's tumbling over at my feet, his blood soaking right through my clothes and him holding in his guts and screaming, God help me, but even God couldn't.
Donna:	Poor John.
David:	Should've been me.
Donna:	Stop being morbid. I love you.

David:	You got lousy taste.
Donna:	Goddammit, David, you piss me off sometimes.
David:	*(pause)* Maybe some things you don't understand.
Donna:	Tell me what I don't understand.
David:	The war.
	(Here the tape runs out.)

*

Fragment of a loose note (found in David's journal), 6 August 1969

. . . Repeating nightmare: I'm lying on my bed and I see her, she has a long sleek braid of black hair, black shirt and trousers. I want her, I sit up, take her wrists, hold them while I kiss her, and then I have her on the bed, I'm on top of her, hands under her blouse, on her breasts, and we're lying on the ground caked with huge rotting leaves where it's so fucking hot, she's screaming, I'm pushing her legs apart, I'm inside her and sobbing goddammit, John's dead, and she's crying too because I'm fucking her so damn hard, and finally I stop, but I can't stop crying. She's still, breathing, the only one left alive. Her whole family shot dead. Red gloves on my hands: blood.

*

WAR STORY
(Conclusion)

Heather slipped her body off like an old coat, one too heavy for summer. She felt nothing, only that she had managed to become invisible, which was why she had come to the island in the first place. Life moved through her like the sails of boats that dipped and swayed through air. She would occasionally sleep with Bill and socialize with him and his friends. It didn't matter. She had no body to protect from them or to feed or shelter from the elements.

She became wind and rain, the power of this energy falling on Bill's skin. No doubt this change of form awed and humbled him, which was why he said to her over a drink, I'm sorry about what happened with Mike. Heather did not have to answer, only fall on Bill with the quiet of an afternoon shower, only be the damp coastal air that the people of the island wear like summer clothing. It was nothing more than Bill's illusion that his hand lifted her chin, that his lips touched hers, that later he drew her to him and she responded to the touch of his hands, which were interchangeable with any hands, which could have belonged, maybe did belong, to Mike. It never happened; he only imagined that the core of her shuddered to his voice whispering in her ear, I'm leaving for Nam real soon, his body pulling hers into the undertow of war.

It never happened because she'd gone to air, leaving by the window, scudding along the beach through scavenging gulls, candy wrappers, cigarette butts, leaving behind Bill, Mike, an army of them in the depths of her body. Much later, she opened her eyes to the whiteness of the sky over the beach, a wall of fog where Bill hung like a picture, looking down at her. You're good stuff, he said. One helluva fuck. She thought she heard echoes, many voices in the bed with her where she floated bodiless above the water. The wind and rain blew hard and bitter now as she stared into Bill's face.

You're not coming back from Vietnam, she heard her body say. You're going to die. Bill's skin went the grey of a storm. He lifted his hand and slapped her hard. All he struck was air. She'd left through the sky, to be sure she'd get away. Now she moves through the bending of space into wartime, the random speeding and slowing of clocks to the moment of death, which is everywhere and always now. It was the end of her sanity, knowing who would be injured and broken, who would die when.

*

Tape Transcript #3 (excerpt), 14 August 1969

David: I keep having nightmares. You got that damn thing on?

Donna: Just think of it as a conscience. It's always on.

David: Don't have a conscience.

Donna: You don't talk when I've got it off, either. Pretend this record is history. History wants a piece of us. History's a fisherman reeling us in on tape.

David: Got his hooks in us. You want more than that?

Donna: Your human version of the war, that's all.

David:	You know everything, Donna. That's what your story says. "Who would be injured and broken, who would die when."
Donna:	The girl in the story said it to warn me. It was the end of her sanity, knowing it.
David:	And you still want to know more.
Donna:	She wasn't a twin. I come and go inside of you.
David:	No, Donna, you don't.
Donna:	Yes I do. And I feel you in me. At the piano, in my hands.
David:	You don't want to feel what's in my hands. You'll get sick again.
Donna:	Sick of not knowing. Sick of living with signs and images, not even music.
David:	I think I'm afraid to talk.
Donna:	You're still my brother. Whatever happened, I'll forgive you.
David:	You mustn't, no one has the right.
Donna:	God does.
David:	You're not God. Anyway, God won't.
Donna:	Don't say that, David.
David:	I torched a village. I took my fucking rifle and shot them all dead, day after they killed John. Six of us, and one girl left alive, hiding in the bushes, a shit-scared look on her face, so I went and drew my bayonet like this, see, and I said come here, honey, and you know what I went and did to her?
Donna:	Shut up, David, I don't want to hear about this.
David:	I was last, when I was done with her, I killed her.
Donna:	Oh God, stop it, stop.

David: You still want to forgive me?
(*We were both crying. Sound of the tape recorder being turned off.*)

*

15 August 1969

Dear David,
I still want to forgive you.

I decided to write it down on paper so you can read it again and again.

I took very seriously what you said, and it upset me. That is the other reason why I am writing a letter. I need some physical distance. I can't talk to you right now inside the space we've shared all our lives, the one in which you've rearranged the furniture and drawn the shades against the light. It's my space too, and I feel shamed by the darkness of it, as if I were somehow involved in what you did, as if I'd been sheltering a secret inside of me, letting it rest in the silence of things imagined.

I remember what you said about my knowing everything, a sense you had of premonition in that story. I hadn't felt that. We'd said we'd talk and write, and the story was my way of uncovering the meaning of my own experience. Since our conversation, I've begun to think there must be more to it than that. A sentence speaks across the distance between us, but then it sets up strange harmonics, humming across time like a telephone wire with a thousand conversations that we don't recognize. Somewhere among these voices was your own, and I must have heard it. And if you hadn't been so inundated by the war, my story would live in the muscle and bone of your body, as yours does in mine. How well we know each other, David. How well we all know everything.

You have to live with what you've done, you will have to find a way to atone; I realize both these things. Only you can't carry this awful load all by yourself. We've always been close, so please don't push me away. And even if you don't feel comfortable talking about this to Mother and Dad (which I can understand), they'd get you some help to sort things out; they've always said they would. Please ask them, David; don't be afraid.

Will you call and let me know you got this? If I don't hear from you, I'll come by and knock on your door.

I don't know why it happened, I wish it hadn't. I know you're thinking this also.

Donna

The note David left, 15 August 1969

Please burn all my papers, Donna. God does not forgive everything.

Sorry to end this way.

D.

Donna's journal, 25 August 1969

David never saw that letter I wrote. It was the talking that did him in, his hearing it. The sound of his voice went off inside his head, a shot.

I found him.

Home now, listening to the Bach B-Minor Mass. John's parents came to visit, along with friends my brother

forgot he had. I have been going for walks, trying to sleep.
Mother and Dad sit on the white porch. They don't speak.
Sea-wind breathing on them, the only sound.

*

Donna's journal, 25 August 1970

A year has passed, and I'm going to Europe to complete my
studies in music. Quiet grief like sea air; the house has
been damp with it. My parents can't talk about David.
They want me to leave home, to get away from the chill
cold of everything that's happened. I never will. David
was my twin; his footsteps echo where I walk.

My brother and I were close to each other when his
life was good, before the war put an end to that. So in his
memory I want to write a story about goodness, one I will
leave for my parents. I'm thinking of the natural goodness
of things, how young animals frisk and play and chase each
other, how they shape their bodies for adulthood, for
leaping and bounding to the hunt, for mating and dying.
And all the while, they know nothing about what is to
come. Maybe innocence would be a better word for this,
not goodness.

It's our eighteenth birthday. In Meredith Point,
the spring air's warm and the water at its rising tide is still
too cool for a swim. The two of us are down at the beach
with school friends. My brother goes charging straight
into the sound, T-shirt on, jeans rolled up, kicking and
splashing the water. David's got his back to us, he's flexing
his arms, you can tell he's laughing, showing off, pretending not to feel the cold. Go on, man, all the way, John yells.

Because his back is turned, David can't see John charging like a stallion along the water's edge, then swooping down so that his long arms scoop up Niagara Falls and dump what looks like a bucketful on David's back. David jumps, arms flailing. John yells "Man overboard!" as my brother loses his footing and tumbles into the waves like a stone-drunk sailor. Soaking wet, he rights himself and comes bounding out of the water, leaps on John and shoves him in. They're like a pair of wet pups roughing it up, bobbing on the waves. David on John's shoulders, then John on David's, two happy guys, John alive in his young, beating drum of a body. And right across the beach you can hear David's laughing, all sharps, major scales, wild, bright arpeggios shivering the air.

*

Epilogue: Now

How, if ever, the story ends:

Not endings, transformations: the endless loop of matter into energy. Flame hissing at the tip of a match, notes crying out from the tips of her fingers. Donna imagines fire, kinetic as music is. Fire, the teller of stories in cinder and ash.

There is such a thing as having too much history, she thinks. Yet she never thought to honour David's wish, to burn these papers, sure that fire would be another kind of death. Only now she's read him into her body, felt her brother seeing with her eyes. This is what language does, and fire cannot change that.

Yet she has also read herself into the world that is

burning, into Kuwait and Baghdad and tomorrow somewhere else, a story told from the point of view of fire. The past melting into now like candle wax into the heat of flame, into the crack and bang of kindling wood that is at once the sound of David's bullet and the terror of the war that always is. No beginning or end of it. Her papers tell her time does not exist, time is a lie tattooed on decades as numbers are on prisoners: the forties, the sixties, the nineties. As if her father's war were not, in some way, David's, were not a part of human devastation, a common fire.

Try that lie on your father, she thinks, and on your mother also. Beat it out to John on drums, repeat it to your brother David and to the innocent girl he killed in the fever of Vietnam; tell it to the human soul which suffered so unutterably in them all. Tell them they are severed by time; they do not burn inside us. Tell them how much we deny.

The prime-time video war made fireproof. Now that we'll believe.

Truth says remember the dead. Burn everything.

This is why Donna will destroy these papers. She will let fire tell what happened, what is still happening. She wants a bonfire, a hearth that is like the body's warmth, a paradox: a resting-place of stories, a hope of life born dancing on the grave.

Her brother waits inside her hands.

She strikes a match.

This is the way the story ends: it never ends. It changes form, it is a fire on the earth. It lives.